Norman Schnurman,
Average Person

Norman Schnurman,
Average Person

Jean Davies Okimoto

G. P. Putnam's Sons
New York

J

c. 1

ACKNOWLEDGMENTS

I would like to thank the following people for their help with *Norman*:
N. H. Davies, Sergeant M. E. "Mike" Dowd, Executive Director of the Denver Police Athletic League, Les Sample of the Sample Book Shop, Katie Kirkman, Steve Okimoto, Amy Kirkman, Dylan Okimoto, P. C. Kirkman, Evie and Hugh Murray, the halfback for John Ralston's San Lorenzo High football team, vintage '53, Joltin' Joe, D.B.R. II, and the Bitch and Moan Society.

—*Jean Davies Okimoto*

Library of Congress Cataloging in Publication Data
Okimoto, Jean Davies.
Norman Schnurman, average person.
Summary: A sixth grader who doesn't like sports wishes
he could find something to do that would make his dad, a
former college football star, proud of him.
[1. Fathers and sons—Fiction] I. Title.
PZ7.0'415No 1982 [Fic] 82-9045
ISBN 0-399-20913-1 AACR2

APR '83

For my mother and father, Edie and Norm

Norman Schnurman,
Average Person

1

I was real happy the afternoon that P.W. and I went to Reasonably Honest Al's. But when I think about it now, if I had known then what was going to happen that day—I wouldn't have been so happy.

But I was happy about everything in my life, except my name, which was no big deal because I'm never happy about my name. My name is Norman Schnurman and I wish it weren't. It's not that I mind Schnurman too much, but I wished my parents had named me something besides Norman.

My friend P.W. Wilcox knows I don't like my name. P.W.'s real name is Peter Wilcox but everyone calls him P.W. which stands for pussy willow. That's because he stuck some pussy willows up his nose in the second grade and he had to go to the emergency room at Harborview Hospital to get them out. P.W. and I and one other person are the only guys in our sixth-grade class who don't like sports. It doesn't matter too much for P.W. because he plays the cello in the Junior Symphony. I've noticed that when you do stuff like that no one cares if you're crummy at sports.

The other person in our class who hates sports is Nathan Beekin. He has three hundred and seventy-one pimples and holds the class championship for nose picking. Nathan Beekin is actually a rather gross person. Besides Nathan, P.W. and me, I guess there are a few girls in our class who don't like sports. One of them is Debbie Chin. She looks pretty good and her hair goes way down her back. I liked her in the fourth grade but I never told anyone, not even P.W. Debbie Chin is the only girl in the class shorter than me. When we have square dancing in P.E. I always hope I get her for a partner. There's nothing worse than when they say, "Swing your partners—do-si-do," and there I am with my nose in some girl's navel.

Square dancing I don't hate as much as the other stuff we do in P.E., but everyone would think I was really weird if they knew that. Norman Schnurman, Square Dance Hero—that doesn't sound too exciting.

I wouldn't mind the name Schnurman if people called me "Mean Joe Greene Schnurman" or maybe something like "Muhammad Ali Schnurman." My Dad has a sports nickname and a lot of people still call him it even though he is almost forty years old. My Dad is Mad Dog Dave Schnurman and that makes a big problem for me, Norman Schnurman, who hates all sports—especially football. Dad was the star running back for the University of Washington Huskies in 1963 and he held the rushing record for fifteen years. The team mascot is a Husky dog and sometimes the team is called the Dogs. They say my Dad used to rush like a mad dog and that's how he got the name Mad Dog Dave Schnurman. It seems like my Dad still talks about football all the time.

P.W. and I were talking about football too, this afternoon, but it was sure not in a way that my Dad would have liked. P.W. and I were riding our bikes down Rainier Avenue to Columbia City where they have some secondhand stores. I always like to inspect the merchandise and check on prices. I like junk a lot.

We rode past the football field at Rainier playfield and at least three Junior Football League teams were out there practicing. It was a real hot day and it seemed more like summer even though it was September already.

"It must be hot with all those pads and helmets on," P.W. said, looking over at the guys on the field.

"I know. It sure seems dumb on a hot day to put on all that stuff and then go out in the dirt and jump on each other."

"Dumb on a cold day too," P.W. said. "I wouldn't want to be the guy on the bottom with my face in the dirt and some sucker's foot in my ear."

"Me either—and those shoes have cleats. A person could get hurt playing that game."

11

I actually don't consider myself a coward, it's just that I'm not crazy about pain. P.W. understands that because he's like that too.

We stopped at the corner and waited for the light to turn green.

While we were waiting, I looked back at the field and for a minute I thought I was seeing things. There was this man standing by one of the teams and I thought it was my Dad. I looked at my watch—it's a Mickey Mouse watch that I got at a garage sale. It keeps real good time and I only paid seventy-five cents for it. Well, anyway, my watch said 4:30 and my Dad's always still at work at 4:30 so I knew I must be wrong. The guy that looked like my Dad was way over on the other side of the field and I couldn't really see him that well. I didn't know what my Dad would be doing hanging out around a Junior Football League team, anyway— so I just forgot about it.

The light turned green and P.W. and I rode across the street and down to Reasonably Honest Al's. I've been going to Reasonably Honest Al's store about once a week since the beginning of third grade. That's when my Mom first let me ride my bike down Rainier Avenue. Al's a pretty nice guy and he has all kinds of stuff in his store. It's divided into two parts. One part has all of these old washing machines, dryers, stoves and stuff. I don't know if they really work, but Al says they do. The other part in the back of the store has furniture, old clothes, books, records, bikes, toys—just about anything a person could want. Reasonably Honest Al's is a good place for old comic books too, and that's what P.W. and I wanted to look at today.

12

When we went in the store Al was over in the part with the washing machines. He was all bent over this clothes dryer with his head stuck in it and his rear end sticking out.

"That you, Norman?"

"Hi, Al. Yeah, it's me and P.W."

"I got some new merchandise in the back—take a look." Al kept talking to us with his head stuck in the dryer. He has a low voice anyway, but it kind of echoed from being in the dryer. To be polite about it, I would say Al has a weight problem. Actually, Al is a big fat guy and his rear end matches the rest of his body. I think I'd rather have a conversation with a person's face instead of with their head stuck in a dryer and all you talk to is their rear end, if you know what I mean.

"Go on back, Norman," Al yelled again from the dryer.

"Okay, Al. Thanks."

P.W. and I walked to the back part of the store. Al kept all the used books and comic books in the back corner all piled up on a table.

"Wonder if he's got any *Donald Duck*s in?" P.W. asked. P.W. collects *Donald Duck* comic books, but only those printed before 1960. He has over fifty of 'em and if you want to know—they're worth a whole lot of money.

"Looks like there's a box of comics here that Al hasn't even gone through yet."

"Good." P.W. sounded excited. "That means no one else has either."

P.W. sat down on the floor and took the comics one by one out of the old cardboard box. P.W. is real careful with the merchandise. He says one of the

13

reasons his *Donald Duck* collection is worth so much money is because all the covers are on and none of the pages are torn or scrunched up or anything like that. P.W. has never exactly told me the exact amount of money his *Donald Duck* collection is worth. He says it's not quite as much as a *Superman* collection would be, but still a lot of money. I'm sure P.W. is right about this because P.W. is real smart.

While P.W. went through the comics, I decided to look around and see what other new merchandise Al had gotten in. I noticed some strange-looking lamps over in the corner on another table across from where the books were.

There were three of these lamps, all alike. Al must have gotten a good price on 'em to get three of a kind. They were made out of this real shiny ceramic stuff and they were these hula ladies with grass skirts made out of real straw like a broom and they had no clothes on the top. And they had these two light bulbs sticking out of their chest and when you turned on the switch the light bulbs lit up.

"Hey! P.W." I said. "You gotta see these lamps!" I tried all the switches on all the lamps and they all lit up exactly like the first one I tried. P.W. put the comic books down and came over where I was fooling around switching on the hula-lady lamps.

"Here, P.W. Watch this!" I switched on the lamp and P.W. laughed and he wanted to try it. He switched it on and then I switched it on after him, only I guess I got kind of clumsy. Also, I was poking P.W. and he'd punch me and laugh when the lamps turned on and we were kind of jumping around and punching each other—just fooling around and switching on the lamps—when I tripped and fell into the table.

All three of those lamps crashed over and fell down on top of me where I had landed on the floor under the table.

"Norman Schnurman! What's that noise?" Al must have heard the crash even though he sounded like he had his head still stuck in the dryer. And he sure moves fast for a big fat guy because he was halfway across the store in just a few minutes standing over me and glaring down.

There I was with a bunch of half-bare hula ladies with light bulbs sticking out their fronts and falling-apart broom hula skirts all broken up and all over me. I even had some of those straw skirt pieces stuck in my hair. I couldn't see Al's face real well from where I was on the floor because from where I was, I could only look up at him and get a view of his stomach hanging over his pants. Al really should go on a diet, but I didn't think this would be a very good time for me to suggest it to him, what with me sitting in a pile of his brand-new, three-of-a-kind, busted-up merchandise.

"Norman, I'm gonna get you a broom and a bag and you can clean up all them lamps. You can keep 'em and maybe some of 'em can get theirselves glued back up 'cause Norman, you just went and bought yourself three gen-u-ine Hawaiian hula-girl lamps." Al sounded real matter-of-fact and not too mad, but I knew he meant business, too. Al went on telling me about the deal I had just made buying these broken lamps. "Now, Norman, I know these lamps coulda gone for five bucks apiece, but since you're such a regular customer and all, for you— you can have all three of 'em for four bucks apiece. That comes to twelve dollars and I'll expect you to pay it off at a rate of two dollars a week. Think you can handle that, Norman?"

"Yeah, Al, that'll be okay and uh . . . I'm ah . . ." I was feeling real stupid at this point and didn't quite know how to tell him I felt bad.

"What is it, Norman?"

"I'm sorry, Al."

"It's okay, kid. Maybe if you glue 'em real good you can get 'em to work again."

Al went and got the broom and the bag and P.W. helped me put the pieces in the bag. One of the lamps only had its head off and looked like maybe it could get glued back together, but the other two looked pretty hopeless.

"Too bad about the lamps, Norman," P.W. said as he held the bag open.

"Yeah."

"Too bad that you gotta pay twelve dollars for broken stuff."

"Yeah."

"Guess we better get going."

"Yeah."

P.W. and I got on our bikes and started riding away up Rainier Avenue. Al waved good-bye and P.W. waved back, but I couldn't because I was riding one-handed and holding the bag in my other arm.

I didn't know what I was going to do with the

lamps, even if I did get one head glued back on and the straw stuck back for the skirt. It wasn't the kind of lamp I could give my Mom for her birthday or for Mother's Day, and if I kept it myself, I know Sally would make a big deal and get on my case about it.

Sally is my sister. She's sixteen and I know she'd make a big deal about that lamp because one time I had a poster in my room that I got at a garage sale of this lady with a wet shirt, and she was real pretty and you could see right through the shirt. Sally bothered me a lot about that. She'd say over and over in this stupid voice, "Oh, Norman! Norman's got a poster! Norman's got a poster!" I got sick of Sally saying that, so I finally took the poster down and put up a poster of a baboon. The baboon had this funny smile on its face and it was wearing a white shirt only it wasn't wet. I gave the poster of the lady to P.W. and he keeps it in his closet because his Mom doesn't like him to have stuff like that and she snoops around his room a lot.

We rode by the football field, but I guess the football practice was over because the only people there were a couple of men jogging around and a lady with a dog.

We got to P.W.'s house first because his house is closer to Rainier Avenue than mine. P.W. lives on 32nd Street and I live two blocks away on 34th Street. I first met P.W. in the second grade at the bus stop on the first day of school. We've been friends ever since. P.W. moved to our neighborhood, which is the Mt. Baker area of Seattle, from Bellevue, where he used to go to Eastgate Elementary School. Everyone in P.W.'s family plays some kind of instrument. His family is practically a whole band. My sister, Sally, is wonderful at music, too. Sally plays the piano and sings real good. Everybody says Sally sings like Julie Andrews, and every year she always gets the lead part in the school musicals and the plays, too. And when the high-school choir has a concert and it's time for someone to sing a part all by themselves, they always pick my sister. Sally gets straight A's and besides that, everybody says she's real beautiful. I guess you would say my sister, Sally Schnurman, is a star. The only instrument I can play is the kazoo.

P.W. put his bike in the garage and walked up to the house.

"So long, Norman. See you tomorrow."

"Yeah. 'Bye, P.W." I got on my bike and started to head home.

"Norman?" P.W. yelled after me.

"Yeah?"

"How are you gonna get the twelve dollars?"

"I dunno. Guess I'll have to try and figure something out."

"Yeah. Well, 'bye."

On the way home I thought about my financial situation, which I guess you would say is not real great right now. In fact, I have a pitiful financial situation because I am broke. I made a lot of money this summer mowing lawns, but there has been such good merchandise at the garage sales this fall that I spent it all. I go to garage sales every weekend. Garage sales and video games are what I spend my lawn-business money on.

When I got to my house, my Mom and Dad were

both already home from work 'cause both their cars were in the garage. My Mom works in the loan department at Seattle First National Bank and she also sells Avon stuff on the side, lipsticks and things like that. My Dad is the produce manager at Joe Albertson's Supermarket. I don't know how much he likes his job. Mom told me once that it's hard for him to go to work and be in charge of vegetables when he used to be such a big football star. But he seems real happy this time of year because it's football season and he watches all the games. There's Monday Night Football and Thursday Night Football and then he goes to the Husky games on Saturday and the Seahawk games on Sunday. When they're not having a home game then he watches football on Saturday and Sunday on TV. That's why I'm usually at garage sales.

My father used to try and get me to watch with him, and he also used to take me out in the backyard and try to teach me about it. But he knows I'm no good at it and he hasn't bothered me about it this year. I'm real glad about that.

I went in the house and right up to my room and put the bag of broken lamps under my bed. Mom and Dad were in the kitchen and Sally was in her room on the phone talking to her boyfriend, so no one saw me with the bag.

Sally is a junior in high school and her boyfriend, John Blakely, is a senior. He's also the captain of the football team and he's this big bozo with no neck. I call him Bozo Blakely, but not to his face, mostly only to P.W. My Dad thinks it's just great that Sally has no-neck Bozo Blakely for a boyfriend because of the football and all.

Mom called me for dinner. I guess she had heard me come in.

"Norman—dinner's ready. Wash your hands."

"Okay," I yelled down the stairs. I looked at my hands and they didn't look dirty to me. I wish just for once my Mom would call me for dinner without telling me to wash my hands. You'd think when a person is in the sixth grade that their mother would stop telling them stuff like that. I went in the bathroom and turned the water on and off and went downstairs.

We were having chicken livers in this gooey stuff over noodles. Everybody in the family likes it except me. I sat down and put a very small pile of the stuff on my plate and then started eating the bread. "It's delicious—just like always," my Dad said, smiling at Mom.

"Sure is," Sally said. "Wish I didn't have to eat so fast, but John is picking me up at seven and taking me to rehearsal."

Sally is going to be Annie in *Annie Get Your Gun* and she goes to rehearsal two nights a week from 7:30 to 8:30. Mom and Dad started talking about Sally's play and I kept eating the bread. Then Mom said that she had to go out for a while this evening too because she had to deliver some of the Avon stuff to a customer.

"Well, Norman," Dad said in this real cheerful voice, "that'll leave you and me here after dinner. Do you have much homework?"

"Nope."

"Good. Then we'll be able to sit down and have a talk."

I started feeling a little nervous. I wondered what he wanted to talk to me about. Sometimes both my Mom and my Dad have these big talks with me about my grades because all I ever get is C's and they want me to do better. But no matter how hard I try that's all I get and they keep thinking I'm not trying. I think that they think that if only I tried harder I could get A's like Sally. But I can't because I'm not smart like her. They don't seem to get the idea that when I'm doing my very best I'm still a C person.

But I didn't think my Dad wanted to give me one of his grade lectures because it was only the third week of school and it would be a while before we'd get report cards. His "try-hard-and-you'll-succeed" lecture always came about a day or two after report-card day. I couldn't figure out what he wanted to talk to me about.

Bozo came to pick up Sally and then right after that Mom left. It was my turn to do the dishes so I stayed in the kitchen.

"Norman, when you're through with the dishes come on in the living room."

"Okay."

I rinsed off the dishes and put them in the dishwasher real slow. I wasn't in any hurry to find out what he wanted. My Dad was waiting in the living room and finally he came in the kitchen.

"Norman, what are you doing?"

"Cleaning the sink." I had finished the dishes, but I kept hanging around in the kitchen.

"Oh. Well, it looks clean to me. Come on in and sit down."

21

"Okay." I followed him into the living room and sat down on the couch across from my Dad's chair. He always sits in the same chair, right in front of the TV.

"Norman," Dad began in this serious voice, "my friend Bob Pierce has been transferred to Kansas. He'll be working for the division of the Boeing Company that's in Wichita and he'll be moving next week."

I wondered what his friend moving had to do with me, but I didn't say anything.

"Bob Pierce has been the coach of the Bears, the Junior Football League team in the intermediate-weight division. Bob asked me if I'd take over as coach."

When I heard my Dad say "Junior Football League" my hands started to sweat. I looked down at the floor.

"I went over to their practice today. I left work a little early to check it out. I'll tell you—it sure was great to be on the field again. It's a nice group of boys and I told Bob I'd love to do it." Dad leaned forward in his chair and looked right at me. He sounded very serious, but excited, too. "Norman, I expect you to play on my team. I want you to give it all you've got for one season. I just know that after a really good exposure to the game that you'll love it the way I do."

I started feeling sick and my Dad kept talking.

"With me as coach and being on the team with boys in your weight class, we are going to turn you into a first-rate running back."

"But, Dad—!"

"This is very important to me, Son, and I expect

you to participate. We'll be out there together, Norman, practicing every Monday and Thursday at four-thirty. Twice a week, rain or shine—we'll come to play, as they say!" Dad laughed.

"Dad, I really—"

"I'll be getting off work a little early on those days and I'll swing by the house to change my clothes and pick you up. Norman, just think—we'll be going to the field together. This will be great— just great!" Dad got up out of his chair. "Now, you wait right there, Son—because have I got a surprise for you!"

He ran out of the room almost like he was already on a football field. I heard him in the garage, and when he came back, he had this package.

"Here you go, Norman—catch." Dad grinned as he tossed me the package.

It went right through my hands and landed on the floor. I was so nervous. I wondered how the heck I was supposed to catch a football if I couldn't even catch a package. But Dad didn't even seem to notice.

"Go on, Son. Go on—open it."

My Dad had this big smile on his face. It was awful. I opened it and I just sat there looking at all this football crap. There was this shirt that said "BEARS" on it and it said "BEARS" on the helmet, too. And then there were these shoulder pads and pants and socks with stripes and some other pads, too. He had bought me the whole suit.

Dad walked over to this trophy case we have in the living room that has all his football awards in it. "Look at the back of the jersey, Norman."

I held up the shirt and looked at it. I didn't know

what I was supposed to be looking for. It just looked like a football shirt to me.

"I got number thirty-three for you, Son." Dad talked more slowly now. He was still looking at the trophies. Then he turned toward me. "Thirty-three," he said, real quiet, "that's my old number." His eyes were watery.

2

Dad didn't waste any time trying to turn me into a running back. The very next afternoon he made me help him drag all this crap from the garage onto the front lawn. He set up two lawn chairs, a wheelbarrow and an old tire like an obstacle course.

"Now, Norman, these things will be like the defensive players who are being blocked out of your way so you can run between them. I'll be the quarterback and hand the ball off to you. See that tree over there by the bushes?" he said, pointing to the edge of the lawn.

"Yeah."

"That'll be the end zone. You run there as fast as you can, cutting in and out of the defense."

"You mean the tire and the wheelbarrow and that stuff?"

"Yeah—the defense."

I looked at the junk all over the lawn and I wished I was somewhere else.

"All right, Norman. Now, ready—go!"

Dad handed me the ball and I started to run.

"No. No. Not like that," he yelled. "Come back here." I hadn't even gotten to the wheelbarrow yet. I wondered what I'd done wrong. I walked back to Dad.

"Don't hold the ball like that, Norman. You'll fumble or they'll strip it right out of your hands. Here, look—like this." Dad took the ball and showed me how to hold it. He put it close to his body, with his shoulder turned in. He said I was carrying it like a loaf of bread.

"All right. Now, try it again. Ready . . . Go!"

I ran as fast as I could, trying to remember to hold the ball right. I got past the lawn chair.

"Faster, Norman—faster. Now, cut! Cut! Norman, cut!" I tried to go faster, but I slipped by the wheelbarrow and fell in it.

"Come back here, Norman," Dad yelled.

I got up out of the dumb wheelbarrow. There was some water and leaves in the bottom of it and my pants were wet with the leaves stuck to me.

"Now, this time, work on those cuts and we'll concentrate on the speed later."

I slowed down and made it around the wheelbarrow and the tire, and one of the lawn chairs.

"You're almost in the end zone, Norman. Run! Run!" Dad's voice boomed across the lawn. When I heard him I guess I got shook-up because I slipped again and this time crashed into the lawn chair. It folded up over my leg.

"Okay, Son—go take a shower. That's enough for today. At practice I want you to work hard on your speed and timing." Dad was whistling while he collected the defense and put it in the garage.

I was tired and sore from falling into that junk and I went to bed early that night. But before I went to sleep I kept hearing my Dad's voice in my head yelling at me, over and over again, "Cut, Norman, cut!" and I wondered how I would ever run by real people grabbing at me if I couldn't even make it by a lawn chair.

The next morning there were so many things worrying me when I got on the bus for school that I didn't know which one to worry about first.

There was the lamp problem and the money for Al and the football problem, which is really a problem about me and my Dad. It was hard for me to figure out how he thought he could turn me into a football player after yesterday—and also because in P.E. when we choose up sides, it's always a tie between me and Nathan Beekin for who's picked last.

I wish I could be like P.W. sometimes. He has a permanent excuse from P.E. because his Mom doesn't want his hand to get messed up for his cello playing.

And then sometimes I wish I could be more like Dad. My father, Mad Dog Dave Schnurman, was also captain of the Huskies when they went to the Rose Bowl—of all his trophies, his Rose Bowl one is his favorite. Running backs have to be brave and tough because they always carry the ball and they get jumped on more than anybody. My Dad is a big, strong guy with a lot of muscles and brown hair. Mom is very little, even for a lady, and she has blond hair. I turned out more like her except for the hair, which is brown like my Dad's. It seems like all I have in common with my Dad is brown hair.

I always sit next to P.W. on the bus and this morning he was still wondering about what I was going to do about Al.

"Have you figured out how to get the money?" was the first thing he asked me.

"No, I'm still not sure. I get a dollar a week for allowance, so if I gave that to Al for six weeks that would take care of half of it—but I'd still have to get six more dollars."

"Could you borrow some from your Mom?"

"Well, then I'd have to tell her why and I have enough problems at home already." Right then, I didn't feel like telling P.W. about the football thing so I just let it go at that.

While P.W. and I were talking, two fifth-graders who are real creeps started pushing each other around in the back of the bus. I guess one guy sat on another guy's lunch so he hit him and then a big fight started. The bus driver, Mr. McCabe, yelled at them to cut it out, but they didn't. In fact, the one guy took the other guy's lunch and hit him over the head with it. P.W. and I turned around and watched and so did everybody else on the bus. Everyone was yelling. There was food all over the place and those guys still punching each other. Mr. McCabe pulled the bus over and stopped. Then he went to the back of the bus and pulled the guys apart. They had their sandwiches squished all over them and they were a mess. There was no blood or anything—just mayonnaise and lettuce and mustard and baloney and stuff like that on 'em. Mr. McCabe made one guy come and sit in the front and told the other guy to stay in the back. Then he started the bus again and told everybody to turn around and shut up.

While the bus was stopped during the fight, I looked out the window because we had stopped right in front of this movie theater. It was the kind of theater that only shows movies with naked people in them. We pass it every day on the way to school. There's no one there in the morning, but in the afternoon on the way home from school, there's always a line of people waiting to get in—a bunch of men. P.W. and I tried to sneak in once but the manager caught us and threw us out. I was looking at the posters outside that movie while the fight was going on, when I got this idea about the lamps.

"P.W.," I said, "I think I know how to get the money."

"Yeah—how?"

"Well, I think a lot of the guys in our class might want to see the lamp."

"Yeah—if you fixed it, I bet they would."

"Right, and we could make 'em pay."

"Good idea! A dollar? Then you'd only need six guys."

"No, I think that's too much—maybe twenty-five cents."

"Yeah, but then you'd need twenty-four guys and it might be hard to get that many."

"How 'bout fifty cents and then we could have something else too—like that poster of the lady in the wet shirt."

"Yeah, and, Norman, for ten cents extra, I could do my trick."

I really laughed when P.W. said that and I thought it was a good idea too. P.W.'s trick is that he can light farts. He really can, and I've seen him do it lots of times. He just bends over and holds a match by his rear end. Then he cuts loose and this flame shoots out. It's really great. P.W. said he's done it a lot for the guys in the Junior Symphony when they go on this concert trip they take once a year and stay in a hotel. They do a lot of stuff on those trips. One time P.W. said that the guys in his room put towels under the door and then turned on all the hot water in the bathroom and made the room into a sauna. They also threw water balloons out the window. But the hotel people got mad and said the symphony couldn't stay there anymore. But I think that mostly happened because of the sauna they made and the water balloons and not because P.W. was lighting farts.

Even though the symphony people have all seen P.W.'s trick, not too many people at school have, and I was sure they would pay ten cents extra for it. It's a real good trick. A lot of people are double-jointed and can wiggle their ears or raise one eyebrow, but not too many people can light farts.

"P.W., do you think you could keep it up—I mean, like how many times could you do it in a row?"

"Well, that depends on what I eat—but I could eat a lot of beans, Doritos—you know, stuff like that."

"Yeah, and I could play that song on the kazoo while you do it." Then I sang the song kind of quiet, kind of whispering in P.W.'s ear:

Beans, beans, the musical fruit,
The more you eat the more you toot,
The more you toot, the better you feel,
Eat beans for every meal.

P.W. cracked up and so did I and we were laughing real loud when old McCabe turned around and told us to shut up or he'd split us up too.

"Where should we have the show?" P.W. whispered.

"Well, we could put up our camping tent in the backyard and have it as soon as school gets out and before my Mom gets home from work."

The bus was pulling up at school so P.W. and I decided we'd talk about it later. I felt a lot better now that there was a good plan about how to get that money for Al. And I was pretty sure it would work.

At school Mr. Slezak, our teacher, handed back our spelling tests and I got a C, as usual. I studied real hard for that test, too. Mr. Slezak is a pretty nice teacher, even though everybody calls him Sleazy. I think that's because he always looks kind of rumpled up and his hair sticks out funny. My sister, Sally, had Sleazy when she was in the sixth grade, too, and she got straight A's, as usual.

After Mr. Slezak handed out the spelling words for this week, it was time for the Title I people to leave. There are six Title I people in our class and they leave during reading every day to get special

31

help from this special teacher. Some of them see letters all mixed up and the special teacher helps them with that. Whenever the Title I people leave, I wish I could go with them and get special help. I think my parents wouldn't be bothering me so much about my grades if I got my letters mixed up and could be a Title I person.

In P.E. we had to play dodge ball and today I was picked before Nathan Beekin. P.W. gets to run around the playground during P.E. because there's this state law that says you have to have exercise. So even though he has a permanent excuse from P.E. he's supposed to run around. On rainy days, which is a lot in Seattle, P.W. stays in the classroom during P.E. and he's supposed to do sit-ups.

As I was dodging the stupid ball, I kept wishing I could be out there running around the playground with P.W. There's one thing about dodge ball, though, that isn't as bad as some other sports I know. Because as soon as someone hits you with the ball, you're out and then you get to go sit on the side of the gym. Then you don't have to play again until there's only one person left and they start a new game. I always get hit first which is fine with me because I like being out and sitting around. One time I made a list of all the balls I hate. It included the following balls: base, volley, foot, soccer, dodge, tennis and pickle. The only ball that I don't completely hate is Ping-Pong—even though I can't seem to hit it over the net. But at least when it hits me it does not cause pain like most other balls I know.

After school on the way home on the bus, P.W.

and I made more plans about our after-school project. That's what we called having guys pay to see the half-naked hula-lady lamp and P.W. lighting farts.

"I can come over to work on the project after my cello lesson," P.W. said.

"Okay, and while you're having your lesson, I'll work on gluing the head on the lamp."

"Good. Norman, do you think it'll be kind of dark in the tent?"

"Yeah. I think so—why?"

"Well, if it is kind of dark, it'll make it even better when the lamp lights up—more of a surprise."

"I see what you mean and we could put it on a table with something covering the table. Then I could be under the table with my hand behind it. I could sort of wiggle the hula lady around then *ZAM!* Turn on the light!"

P.W. laughed and kind of bounced up and down on the seat when I said that. I don't know why but we both started bouncing on the seats and then a bunch of other people did too. Then old McCabe started yelling that he'd pull the bus over if we didn't stop. After this morning we knew old McCabe meant that, too.

"Norman, we should have some music for the after-school project."

"You mean while I'm wiggling it around, have music and make it like it's dancing?"

"Yeah, you know—Hawaii music." P.W. started moving his arms around and wiggling on the seat like he was doing the hula. I laughed so much I almost fell outta my seat, and old McCabe started yelling "Shut up!" again and saying he'd pull over. P.W. pulled me back on the seat.

"I don't have any Hawaii music," I told P.W.

"Yeah, but I do. I have a forty-five record of 'Aloha.' "

"You know I've got an old record player that only takes forty-fives that I got at a garage sale. I only paid two dollars and fifty cents for it and it works, too."

"Great. Where could we plug it in?"

"Oh, we'll just hook up an extension cord under the tent to the plug in the basement. We'll need that anyway to make the lamp go on."

The bus stopped at McClellan and 34th and P.W. and I got off. He said he'd bring the record and the poster of the lady in the wet shirt over when he was through with his cello lesson, and I went home to glue the lamp.

I had pretty much forgotten about the football problem until I got home and went up to my room to glue the lamp. But the football suit was on the chair where I'd left it last night. Just looking at it made me feel sick. I had this awful feeling and just stared at it for a few minutes. There was that helmet that said "BEARS" and that shirt with number 33 on it. It made me feel sad about my Dad.

My Dad was going to be a pro football player. After he finished playing for the Huskies at college, he was a first-round draft choice. That means he was one of the players out of all the college players in the whole country that got picked first to be in the pros. My Dad got picked by the Baltimore Colts and he went to Baltimore, Maryland, to be on their team. Only he got hurt real bad in an exhibition game before the real season even started. His knee got all screwed up and he never was quite the same, so the Baltimore Colts had to drop him from their team and he never did get to play with the pros. I didn't know my Dad then because I wasn't born.

I put the helmet and the shirt on and went in the bathroom and looked in the mirror. While I was in there I picked up my Dad's razor and pretended to shave even though the amount of hairs I have on my face is zero. I decided that I looked stupid pretending to shave with this football helmet on so I went back to my room and took the stuff off. I put all the football stuff in my closet.

Then I took the bag with the lamps in it out from under the bed. I was real careful with them and I set all the pieces out around me on the floor. Then I went down to the basement and I got an extension cord and the glue and went back up to my room.

I was starting to figure out how the pieces went together when the doorbell rang and it was P.W.

"Hi, how was your lesson?"

"Fine—here's the record and the poster." P.W. handed me a brown grocery bag where he had rolled up the poster and stuck it in with the record. We went up to my room and I put the poster under my bed. We sat on the floor and started figuring out about the lamps.

We fixed the one that had its head broken off first. It was easy to glue on, too. But one of the lamps was completely hopeless. There were just too many pieces so we put it back in the bag.

The other one was missing the head and both arms. We glued it and then while we waited for the glue to dry, I got the 45 record player and we plugged it in and tried the Hawaii record. It was kind of scratchy but we thought it sounded good enough for our after-school project.

"Let's try the lamps," P.W. said. "I think the glue should be dry by now."

"Wanna try 'em to the music?"

"Yeah, I'll start the record and you wiggle 'em and then turn the switch on at the end of the song."

"Okay."

P.W. turned on the music and I started wiggling the lamp that had only had its head broken off. It worked real good and then at the end of the song I switched it on and the two light bulbs lit up.

"Yea!" P.W. cheered and I did too and then he said to try the other one. P.W. started the music again and I started wiggling the lamp only I guess I jiggled it too much because the arms fell off.

P.W. turned off the record. "Well, I guess that one's no good."

"No, but we still have one good one."

"Yeah, that's for sure!"

P.W. had to leave and my Mom and Dad would be coming home from work soon. Also Bozo Blakely would probably be driving Sally home from school any minute, so I put the lamp away under my bed and put the rest of the stuff in my closet.

P.W. and I had decided to have our after-school project the next day. We thought we would tell some guys in our class about it tomorrow and then after word got around—we'd have it the day after that, too. We'd tell the guys it started at four o'clock. That would give us enough time to get the tent up, put the poster up inside, set up the record player and the table and plug in the extension cord. P.W. said he'd bring a lot of fart food for lunch tomorrow and eat some before the project, too.

Now I felt a little better knowing I could get the money for Al because with an after-school project like P.W. and I had figured out, I was sure that absolutely nothing could go wrong.

3

"Norman! Hurry up or you'll be late for the bus!" Mom yelled down to me from upstairs where she was getting ready to leave for work. Dad and Sally had already gone and I was in the kitchen making an extra sandwich to put in my lunch for P.W. I thought it would be a good idea to bring some extra fart food for P.W. just in case he forgot. I decided raw onion might be good so I was slicing up an onion. The whole sandwich was mustard, bread and sliced onion. But while I was getting the onion cut, it made my eyes start watering real bad.

Mom came in the kitchen. "Norman . . ." She stopped and looked at me funny, then she put her purse down and came over and put her arm around me. "What's wrong, Norman? Are you all right?"

"Sure, Mom—I'm fine." I wiped the tears off my face.

"Honey, are you upset about something?"

"No, I was just cutting an onion, and—"

"What?"

"An onion, cutting an onion."

"Norman, you'll miss your bus—what in the world are you cutting onions for?"

"A sandwich."

"But I told you to put some of the leftover fried chicken in your lunch." Mom sounded like she might be beginning to get kind of mad.

"I did. This is for P.W."

"What's for P.W.? Norman, really. This is ridiculous. Hurry up or you really are going to miss that bus."

"The sandwich, Mom—onion sandwiches are P.W.'s favorite. I decided to bring him one. I'm all done now anyway and I can run to the bus stop. I'll make it."

"All right, dear. I'll see you when I get home from work." Mom kissed me good-bye. "I've got to leave or I'll be late."

Mom left and I threw the sandwich in with my lunch and ran to the bus stop. The bus was just pulling up when I got there so I just made it in time. The only thing was that I forgot my social-studies homework and I knew Mr. Slezak would yell at me for that. I don't forget my stuff as much as some guys I know, but Sleazy always yells at everybody when they forget to bring their homework. I think some people don't do it and just say they forgot. He always marks it down a grade if you're late. But I didn't worry about that too much because I was busy thinking about the after-school project.

39

At lunch I sat with the same people I always sit with. Our table is P.W., Robbie Miller, Matt Sato, Eric Silverman, Henry Williams and me. P.W. and I told the guys about the project.

"Hey, you guys, come on over to Norman's backyard today," P.W. said.

"Yeah, and bring fifty cents," I said.

"How come we should bring fifty cents just to go to Norman's backyard?" Matt asked.

"Yeah—I been in Norman's backyard for nothin'," Henry said.

P.W. and I started laughing and the other guys looked at us like we were crazy.

"Because," P.W. said, "Norman and I have a special after-school project in a tent in his backyard and it's an R-rated project."

"It costs only fifty cents," I said again, to make sure they didn't forget about the money.

Eric looked like he didn't believe us. "How do we know it's really something R-rated?"

"Well, we can't tell you exactly what it is 'cause that would ruin the surprise, but one of the items in the project I have to keep in my closet so my Mom won't find it."

That seemed to make everybody interested, and except for Robbie, who said he had to go to the orthodontist after school, everyone said they'd come.

Henry, Matt and Eric had finished their lunches and went out to mess around on the playground until the bell.

I handed P.W. the onion sandwich. "Here, I made this for you just in case you forgot."

"What is it?"

"It's an onion sandwich."

"What else does it have in it?"

"Nothing."

"Just onions and bread?" P.W. asked.

"And mustard."

"Yuk."

"Well, did you remember to bring any fart food for lunch?"

"Just a lot of Doritos. I couldn't find any beans at home. Besides that, I don't like cold beans."

"So eat the sandwich—you know, in case the Doritos aren't enough."

"Norman, I think I'll wait until right before the project."

"Okay." I put the sandwich back in my lunch bag. Robbie was still at the table and he wanted to know why I was trying to get P.W. to eat the onion sandwich.

"Fart food."

"Fart food? How come you wanna get P.W. to fart?"

"For the project, " I said, munching my chicken.

"You mean you're gonna make guys pay fifty cents to get in a tent where P.W.'s farting?"

"No—not just that. Listen, Robbie, " I said real quiet so no one would hear, "since you have to go to the orthodontist and don't get to come—I'll tell you about the project. But don't tell anybody."

"Okay."

"He lights 'em."

"Yeah, really?"

"That's right. P.W. really lights 'em and this

41

bluish flame goes whoosh, and that's not all . . ."
Then I told Robbie about the other stuff, the poster
and the lamp and all, and he was real disappointed
that he had to go to the orthodontist.

The rest of the day went pretty slow because I
kept thinking about the project, but the afternoon
wasn't too bad. We had square dancing in P.E. and
I lucked out and got Debbie Chin for a partner. As I
mentioned before, Debbie Chin is shorter than me
and she has nice hair and her face looks good too. I
never exactly know what to say to girls, all girls,
even Debbie Chin. It really doesn't seem any easier
to talk to her just 'cause she's short. But I was in a
real good mood, though, because I was excited
about the project, so I decided to try and say
something to her, I wasn't sure what, though.

Debbie and I were promenading around the
square and I finally got up my nerve. "I'm glad I
got you for a partner, Debbie."

"Yeah, that's probably just because I'm shorter
than you." Debbie laughed and smiled at me.

"Yeah . . . I mean, no. Well, not exactly." I felt real
stupid, so I just shut up and that was the end of the
conversation.

I wish I could talk to girls like Eric Silverman
does. He had Beth Wakeland for a partner and they
were both talking and laughing the whole time.
Eric's real tall and so's Beth, and he says he goes
over to her house after school sometimes and he
says they have R-rated afternoons. No one knows if
it's really true or not.

After P.E. we had a movie on the volcano when
Mount St. Helens blew up. I've seen a lot of stuff

about it. We have a book about it at home and I have some ash from it in a plastic bag because they were selling a lot of stuff like that around Seattle after the volcano went off. So I wasn't that interested in the movie. Eric Silverman and Beth Wakeland were sitting in front of me whispering and I started wondering what they really do after school.

If you want to know the truth, I have a G-rated life. It's not even PG—my whole life is just rated G. I have never seen a real-live naked lady in my whole life. I was thinking a lot about this while the movie was showing how volcanoes were formed, and I decided that one thing I could do about the situation would be to hide in my sister's closet. We don't have the kind of family where people run around with no clothes on, or even in their underwear. That's why I got the idea of hiding in Sally's closet and peeking while she got undressed. It seemed like a pretty good idea at the time. I decided I'd do it after P.W. and I got through with our after-school project. Because right now it would make too many things to think about.

Today seemed like it would take forever, but it was finally over and as soon as the bus stopped at 34th and McClellan, P.W. and I jumped off and ran to my house as fast as we could.

The first thing we did was to go down to the basement and get the tent. We carried it out to the backyard and P.W. took it out of this big box it's in while I went to the garage and got the sledgehammer. P.W. had the tent on the grass with all these poles and stakes and things laid out. This tent looked more complicated than I thought.

"Do you know what we do first?" I asked P.W.

"Sure. It's easy." He grabbed a pole and tried to stick it in the ground. "This goes up first."

I made a little hole in the ground with the stake and then I stuck the pole in the hole, and then we put the tent on top of the pole and then the whole thing fell down.

This kept happening quite a few times and I was starting to wonder whether the whole after-school project and the tent would ever get off the ground.

Somehow we finally got it up. Some of the poles were sticking out funny and a few stakes kept coming loose, but at least it was up. I don't know why putting up the tent looks so easy when my Dad does it on camping trips. But it did stay up.

Inside the tent everything seemed just fine. The poster of the lady in the wet shirt was taped up on the side of the tent and right under it was a card table which I had covered with a sheet from my bed. The lamp was on the table and the record player was underneath the table. They were both plugged into the extension cord and we plugged that in through the basement window. I had my kazoo in there too for the music for P.W.'s farting part, and we had a coffee can to collect the money in before the guys went in the tent. P.W. and I had remembered everything.

Matt, Eric and Henry were the first guys to come and at first we were worried that no one else would come and that we'd only make $1.50. But we didn't have to worry too long because right after they came a whole bunch of people came. There were some guys from the other sixth-grade class and

44

even a few fifth-graders. Even Nathan Beekin came. There must have been about seventeen guys in all. A lot of 'em were running around the backyard and wrestling and jumping on each other and stuff.

"We got here first," Matt said.

"Yeah—we get to go in first." Eric looked at the tent. "This better be worth it, Schnurman," and he handed me the fifty cents.

I collected the fifty cents from Matt and Henry too, and they went in the tent. P.W. and I decided to have about three guys at a time in there.

I got under the table and P.W. started the Hawaii music. I wiggled the lady around and at the end of the song, just like we planned, I turned the lamp on and the light bulbs on her front lit up.

The guys all started yelling and clapping and P.W. and I knew the project was off to a great start.

"Now, for ten cents extra," I said, "P.W.'s gonna do a special performance for you."

"I can see P.W. play his cello for nothing," Matt said.

"Yeah, when the orchestra plays at assemblies—it's free." Eric didn't seem too interested.

"It's not the cello, dummy," I said. "Look, just pay the ten cents, and if you don't think P.W.'s performance is worth it, you can have your money back."

They all said okay and I collected the ten cents from each of them. P.W. told them to stand back a little and I started playing the bean song on the kazoo. When I got to the part that goes, "The more you eat, the more you toot," P.W. bent over, held the lighter under his rear end and cut loose. That blue flame went whoosh and the guys all yelled and jumped up and down. The people outside the tent all heard the guys inside cheering and clapping and so when Matt and Eric and Henry got out of the tent and I went out to get some more guys, there was a big long line.

The whole project was a success and the only thing that went wrong was that Nathan Beekin got so excited when he was looking at the poster of the lady in the wet shirt that he leaned on it and the whole tent fell down. Everything was a mess, but it didn't matter because Nathan was in the last bunch of guys to be in the tent so the project was over anyway.

Everybody went home after that and P.W. and I counted the money. It came to ten dollars and ten cents. Seventeen guys had paid the fifty cents and all but one had paid the ten cents to see P.W.'s trick. The one who didn't was Nathan Beekin, 'cause he said he didn't have any more money. P.W. and I let him watch anyway and then he ended up knocking the tent down. That guy is a real jerk.

"Norman, with all this money, you won't have to use much of your allowance to pay Al," P.W. said.

"Yeah—but you should have the money from your trick."

P.W. said "Okay" and I paid him the $1.60 and kept the $8.50. Now I only needed to spend $3.50 from my allowance.

P.W. said he didn't think he could fart so many times two days in a row so we decided not to have the project the next day because the whole thing had turned out so good today.

P.W. went home and then Mom and Dad came home from work and right after that Bozo Blakely brought Sally home. P.W. and I had put all the stuff away and so everything seemed real normal, just like usual, which was fine with me.

The phone rang while I was up in my room counting the money again and I figured it was for Sally because it always mostly is. But then right after that my Dad came up to my room.

"Norman," he said in this serious voice, "I just got a call from Mrs. Beekin, Nathan's mother."

When my Dad said that I started to feel nervous.

"Norman, Mrs. Beekin was very upset. She said there was something going on over here this afternoon that was immoral and involved some kind of dirty peep show. She said she would not allow Nathan to come over here again, since there was no supervision."

I couldn't believe that idiot Nathan Beekin! Telling his mother—of all people, his mother—telling her about our project. That guy was even a worse jerk than I thought!

"Norman, I had no idea what to say to Mrs. Beekin, so I told her I'd look into it. Now, exactly what did go on here this afternoon?"

"Well, see, there was this after-school project, and—"

"A school project? This had something to do with a school assignment?"

"No—we just called it an after-school project."

"Who's 'we'?" Dad wanted to know.

"Me and P.W."

"Did P.W. get you into trouble?"

"No, Dad, nothing like that." I sure didn't want

to put the blame on P.W. One person in trouble was enough. "See, Dad, it was really my problem in the first place." Then I explained about how I'd been to Al's and how I broke all three of the lamps and how I owed all the money and then how I got the idea for the project and all. Then Dad wanted to see the lamp so I took it out of the closet and showed him. I thought he'd be mad about the lamp but instead he seemed mad about some other stuff.

"Norman," he said, sounding upset, "I understand that you boys would have fun looking at this lamp—that's certainly normal. But what is disturbing to me is that you felt you couldn't talk to me or your mother about having broken them. We could have helped you find a better way to earn the money to pay Al back."

Then my Dad sat down on the bed next to me. "It was also wrong to have this sort of thing going on after school without telling us. Your mother and I are responsible for what goes on here, Norman— even when we're not here." Then my Dad said that he was going to talk it over with Mom and they would decide what the consequences would be, which means punishment, and he'd let me know.

As he left my room, he said, "You know, Norman, it's even more obvious to me how much you need to be on the football team. When you start practice next week, I'll feel a lot better knowing you're busy after school and not getting into this kind of trouble."

4

The punishment ended up that I had to go over to Nathan's house and apologize to Mrs. Beekin and show her the lamp so that she'd know exactly what the show was. I never did tell Dad about the poster and P.W. lighting farts so the lamp was all I told her about. I was so embarrassed showing Mrs. Beekin that lamp, I wanted to die. It was the worst punishment I could have had because I was hoping I'd get restricted for a week and then I'd be able to miss football practice—but no such luck.

Besides wanting to die when I had to show Mrs. Beekin the lamp, I also wanted to murder her son, Nathan. As I have mentioned before, I am not a violent person, but it was easy for me to imagine breaking that dumb lamp over Nathan Beekin's head.

As I was walking back home, Nathan came running after me.

"Norman! Wait up!"

I walked even faster and I started swinging the paper bag that I had put the lamp in. Nathan caught up with me and kind of trotted along beside me.

"Listen, Norman—I'm really sorry about my mother."

I still didn't say anything. I just kept walking real fast and swinging the bag.

"Norman. It wasn't my fault. I didn't tell her."

"Yeah, well, who did? A little bird?"

"No, my little brother. I told him all about it and then he told her. I was so mad at him. I wanted to beat him up but he's only five and my mother would kill me if I even touched him."

I quit swinging the bag. It started to seem stupid, everyone wanting to beat up on each other.

"I'm real sorry, Norman," Nathan said again.

"Yeah. Well, okay."

"See ya later, Norman." Nathan turned and started back toward his house. "My Mom doesn't want me hanging around you—so I gotta go."

That made me mad all over again, like I'm some kind of rotten person or something. Not that I want to hang around Nathan Beekin anyway. But it made me mad and I was still mad when I got home. I went up to my room and dumped the stupid bag with the lamp in it in my closet and slammed the door. I heard a crash but I didn't even care.

It was starting to rain and I thought I'd go over to P.W.'s and see if he wanted to watch TV or maybe go down to the pizza place and play some video games.

P.W. and I like to do the same stuff. When we were in the fourth grade, sometimes after school if it was raining we used to fool around with the phone book. We'd look up people who had funny names and then we'd call up and say stupid stuff. Our favorite one to call was this person named Hamburger. We'd always call him up and say, "Hello, Mr. Hamburger. How are your buns?" Then we'd laugh a lot and hang up. I think we drove Mr. Hamburger practically crazy in the fourth grade.

We haven't called people up much lately, though, especially not since they put in video games at the pizza place. Space Invaders and Asteroids are my favorites. I'm not really great at video games but I'm not real terrible either. I usually get around three thousand at Space Invaders.

I went over to P.W.'s and we watched TV. I told him about Mrs. Beekin calling up my Dad. I told him that Nathan told his little brother and his little brother had told their Mom.

"Was your Dad real mad?"

"Yeah."

"What happened?"

"He made me go over to Mrs. Beekin and apologize and tell her what the show was and show her the lamp."

"You had to show Mrs. Beekin the lamp!"

"Yeah."

"Did you have to tell her about me lighting farts?" P.W. seemed worried.

"No. I didn't tell my Dad about that stuff."

"Thanks." P.W. didn't seem worried anymore.

While we were watching TV, I decided to tell P.W. about the football problem, although I knew this was one problem that he couldn't help me with— not like how he helped me with the after-school project.

"That's really too bad that he says ya gotta do it," P.W. said. "Do you think there's any way you could get out of it?"

"I've been trying to think of something. But all I can think of is to break my arm or my leg or something."

"How could you do that?"

"I don't know, and I think it's a dumb idea anyway."

"Yeah. It's dumb. One time I heard about this guy who jumped off his garage with a Superman suit on and he broke his leg only he wasn't trying to break his leg he was trying to fly." Then P.W. looked at me real seriously. "Norman, couldn't you just tell your Dad 'no'?"

"Well—I guess I'm scared to do that. It's such a big deal to him. He gave me his old number and everything and also he's mad about the project. He thinks playing football will keep me out of trouble."

"Geez—it's not like you're a crook."

"I know, but if I do this maybe I could get my Dad to be proud of me."

P.W. didn't say anything and I wanted to quit talking about it. I wouldn't have to actually get out there until Monday and at least the weekend was coming and I could do my favorite thing which is go to garage sales.

As it turned out, on the weekend the garage sale was really great and I was glad about that because it took my mind off football.

I had seen the signs for the garage sale on telephone poles and trees and I wrote down the address. I have a special book that I put all the garage-sale information in whenever I see garage-sale signs.

This one was over on 33rd Street and the sign said it started at nine o'clock. The next morning I got there exactly at nine on the dot because I like being one of the first people there. I also had written down the addresses of two other garage sales that I had seen signs for, so I knew it would be a big day.

I usually don't shop for anything in particular except I'm always on the lookout for stuff for my collections. I collect bubble-gum cards and I have collections of *Superman, Empire Strikes Back, Close Encounters of the Third Kind, Star Wars*, and the Beatles. I have two non-reissue Bowman Bubble Gum cards of the Beatles that I bought for two cents apiece and they're worth two dollars apiece now. I like having stuff that nobody wants that is valuable only nobody knows it.

I went in the garage and looked around. They had stuff on tables and out on their lawn too. There were a lot of clothes, some picture frames, a bunch of kitchen junk, a couple of bikes, an old TV, some jewelry and a whole table of records, books and jigsaw puzzles. There was a shoe box of gum cards on the table with the books and I started looking through them first.

More people started to come, and as I was looking through the gum cards, this girl came over to the table where I was and started looking through the records. I kept looking through the cards, but I could see her out of the corner of my eye. She was real pretty. She looked about my age and she had on a T-shirt that said "SEATTLE PEOPLE DON'T TAN—THEY RUST!" She looked at the records real carefully, looking on the back at the dates. There was an old man looking at a pile of gardening tools and she called to him.

"Gramps, they're over here."

The old man came over. He was tall and had very white hair. "Any good years?" he asked her.

"Not much before 1970."

"How much do they want for them?" The old man looked for a price sign.

"There was a sign on the top of the pile—it said two dollars and fifty cents apiece."

"Kind of high, don't you think?" the old man said. Then he went back and looked at the gardening tools and she went with him. When I looked around, they had gone. I finished going through the cards and I found two *Star Wars* cards that I bought for a penny apiece. I think that someday *Star Wars* gum cards are going to be worth a lot of money, especially since it was the first movie like that.

I checked my book for the address of the next garage sale, got on my bike and left. Two *Star Wars* cards for a penny apiece seemed like a good start.

I rode over to 42nd Street where they really had a lot of stuff. It looked like several families had gone in on it together. They had tables with lots of clothes piled on them. Nothing there looked interesting so I went over to where they had books and records.

There were two people at that table and it was the same girl and the same old man from the other garage sale.

"Hi." She looked up from the records and smiled. I guess she had recognized me from the other garage sale.

I said "Hi" back and then I started looking through the books. I felt kind of embarrassed, but I don't know why. She was so pretty.

The old man went and looked at some yard furniture, and then she went and looked at the clothes. When I looked up, they were gone again. I wished I had said something to her besides "Hi."

They didn't have any gum cards but there was a model airplane that looked like it had all its pieces and it was only twenty-five cents. It seemed like a real good bargain and sometimes I like to make models, so I got it. I just love a good bargain.

My sister, Sally, used to call me Oscar for that fuzzy guy on *Sesame Street* who lived in a garbage can and loved trash. I am kind of a junk junkie but the stuff I like isn't trash. It's all good stuff. I checked my book for the address of the next garage sale and left. I usually take a backpack with me to put the merchandise in, and so far I had one model airplane and two *Star Wars* cards in my backpack. There was still lots of room for more merchandise.

The next garage sale was on this street called Dose Terrace. As soon as I got there, who should I see but the girl and the old man. We all laughed and I said, "It must seem like I'm following you."

"No, we've all just studied where the good sales are today," the old man said. Then he shook my hand. "I'm Lars Koski," he said, "and this is my granddaughter, Carrie Koski."

"Hi, I'm Norman Schnurman."

"We just moved in," Mr. Koski said. "Do you live in this neighborhood?"

"Yeah, I've lived in Mount Baker my whole life."

"It seems real nice." Carrie smiled. "Do you always go to garage sales or are you looking for something special today?"

"I go almost every weekend. I'm kind of hooked on 'em."

Mr. Koski and Carrie laughed, "We are, too," he said. "It's kind of our hobby."

Then we talked more and I found out that Carrie was in the sixth grade, too. She asked me where I went to school.

"Evergreen."

"Evergreen—that's the school I'm supposed to go to. What's it like?" Carrie asked.

"Oh, it's okay, I guess."

"I'm kind of scared to start a new school, if you want to know the truth."

"Yeah, well, I could . . . ah . . . you know . . . sort of show you around."

"I'd like that—thanks, Norman." Carrie smiled.

It seemed real easy to talk to Carrie Koski even though she was so pretty. Maybe it was because she liked garage sales too.

Her grandfather went to look at the tools and Carrie and I went to where they had a table of books and records.

"Gramps is so friendly," Carrie said. "I always

meet people 'cause of him. Sometimes it gets a little embarrassing, though, because he's always going up to perfect strangers and getting in these conversations."

"Does he live with you?"

"Yeah. He lives with me and my Mom. Gramps is retired. He used to be a crab fisherman in Alaska."

"Did he have his own boat?"

"Yeah, but he sold it when he retired, and he helped Mom buy the house we just moved into."

"Does your Dad live with you?" I asked.

"Nope. He's dead." Carrie said that real matter-of-fact and I didn't know what to say.

"I didn't mean to sound nosy," I said, "but that's too bad about your Dad."

"It's okay." Carrie leafed through the records. "He died when I was a baby. He was killed in Vietnam."

"Oh." I wondered what it would be like not to have a father at all. Most of the people I know who don't have a father living with them, was because their parents were divorced and not because their father was dead.

Carrie looked through the records and I looked through the books. I was thinking about Carrie not having a father when I saw this book called *Winning Through Intimidation*. It was only a quarter and on the front it said, "Read this book and start winning today." I turned it over and read the back cover.

If you've ever found yourself coming out on the short end of the stick, you'll appreciate the rewards that can be yours when you take the initiative in every area of your life.

Learn to deal from a position of strength.

Start WINNING THROUGH INTIMIDATION today.

I was reading the back cover when Carrie's grandfather came over.

"What do you have there, Norman?" he asked.

I showed him the book.

Mr. Koski read the front cover and the back cover. Then he leafed through it and read a few pages. "I'd offer them ten cents for it," he said. "Of course, if they won't go down that low, you could try and settle on fifteen." Mr. Koski handed the book back to me.

I decided to buy the book and I took Mr. Koski's advice on bargaining for it. I did just what he said and offered them ten cents. They didn't go for that but then we settled at fifteen cents. It worked real good.

After I bought the book I talked to Mr. Koski and Carrie some more.

I found out that Mr. Koski and Carrie collect stuff too. Carrie collects teddy bears, *Wonder Woman* comic books, and Beatles records, and Mr. Koski collects buttons from political campaigns, but only the people who didn't get elected. I asked him about this.

"Well, everyone remembers who won. But the people who ran and lost get forgotten, and I like to remember them."

"But they lost."

"Only the election," Mr. Koski said, and I wondered what he meant by that. It sure was nice to talk to him and Carrie. I had to get home but if it wasn't for that I think I would have been happy to hang around with them all day.

I went home and decided to read up on the *Winning Through Intimidation* book. Maybe it would help me get ready for Monday. I was really dreading Monday except for one thing and that one thing was Carrie Koski. It would be her first day at school and I, Norman Schnurman, would get to show her around.

5

Sunday night at dinner the whole family seemed interested in the football thing. My Mom had even made my favorite dinner which is hamburgers and french fries because she said she wanted me to be feeling good for my first football practice.

"Norman," Dad said, "Mom and I are going out to a movie tonight and I'm going to leave the Bears playbook with you to look over."

"Pass the french fries, please," I said.

"Norman, did you hear me?"

"Uh-huh."

"After we get home from the movies we can go over it."

Sally reached for the catsup. "It sure is neat that you're going out for football, Norman."

"Mustard, please," I said.

Sally handed me the mustard. "I'm going to study over at John's house tonight, Norman, and if you want—I can ask him to stop in when he brings me home and he could help you with the playbook."

"Catsup, please." The last thing I wanted was help in football from no-neck Bozo Blakely.

"Would you like John to help?" Sally asked again.

I took a bite of my hamburger. "No thanks."

"Norman, don't talk with your mouth full," Mom said. Then she asked me if I had tried on the uniform my Dad got me.

"Uh-huh."

"How'd it fit?"

"Okay, I guess."

"It sure will be nice to watch you play football, Norman. John and I could come to one of your games. After all—you've been coming to my musicals all these years."

"And I'd love to come too," Mom said.

"How's the play?" I asked.

"Playbook, Norman," my Dad said, "it's not a play—it's a book of the plays that the Bears use. It has diagrams of what each player is—"

"No, I mean Sally's play—you know, *Annie Get Your Gun.*"

"Oh, well, it's two weeks from Saturday night."

"How are the rehearsals going, dear?" Mom asked Sally, and I was glad to get them talking about her stuff. The football conversation was not making me happy. The last thing I wanted was to have my whole family come and watch me make a fool of myself. It would be bad enough in front of the other guys on the team and in front of my Dad.

Mom and Dad went to the movies and Sally left with Bozo Blakely. I went up to my room and flopped down on the bed.

The house was quiet with everybody gone and all. It was raining outside and starting to get dark. All I could hear was the rain hitting the window and dripping from the gutters.

Every spring, I always help my Dad clean out the gutters. I climb up on this ladder and get all the leaves and dirt out. One time a dead water rat got stuck in the gutter and I had to pick it up with my bare hands and pull it out with all the leaves. I didn't like doing that at all, but maybe it was kind of brave that I did that. Especially the part when its head was all flopping around.

I was lying there thinking about that dead rat. Maybe that was the one semi-brave thing I have done in my whole life. I started imagining these big headlines: "BOY PULLS RAT FROM GUTTER WITH BARE HANDS." "Man, that's dumb," I said to myself, and I turned over on my back and put my hands under my head and just looked up at the ceiling.

I wished I could find something to do that could make my Dad proud of me that wasn't football. Finally I decided that maybe I could be on the lookout for people to rescue or something like that. I could go down to the beach and hang around the dock in case someone fell in. Or maybe I could go to the park and always be watching all the little kids to make sure none of 'em ran out in front of a car. And then the headlines would say "BOY SAVES LITTLE

KID FROM DROWNING," or maybe if there was a fire in the neighborhood I could run in and get the people out and the headline would say "BOY SAVES PEOPLE FROM FIRE."

I got tired of thinking about this so I finally got the Bears playbook Dad had left for me and I started looking at it.

It wasn't really a book, it was just this folder that had some ditto sheets in it with purple ink. There were twelve pages in all and each page had a diagram on it because I guess there were twelve plays.

I know a little bit about football. I guess you can't be the son of Mad Dog Dave Schnurman all these years and not know some stuff about football. For instance, I know that the team that has the ball tries to get it to the end of the field and they are called the offense. I also know that the team that is trying to stop them from doing that by jumping on them is the other team and that's called the defense. I guess you would say that I have a basic understanding of the game of football.

In the playbook each play had a name or some numbers on the top. I leafed through it and it began looking kind of confusing. There was stuff like "32 dive on two" and "Down and out" and "Button hook" and then some stuff about defensive formation; "5-3-3" was one and then one that said "7 Diamond." There were circles and X's all over the place and I didn't get any of it.

I put the playbook down and then I got the *Winning Through Intimidation* book out of my backpack. In the table of contents it had said stuff like "Laying the Groundwork for Winning" and "My Understanding of Intimidation Pays Off," but when I started to read it the book mainly seemed to be about how this guy made a lot of money in the real-estate business. It seemed like mostly what he did was send out a fancy pamphlet that made him look important and then he went to see people with a whole bunch of secretaries and calculators and stuff with him. Then when he made a bunch of money he got a jet airplane and flew people around in it and he acted important so people would go along with his deals and he got rich.

I had paid fifteen cents for this book and I wished I had my money back. I didn't see how it would help me play football, because I was sure guys wouldn't keep from tackling me just because I tried to look mean and like I was an important football player.

I know it sounds dumb, but even though I was sure that the idea of the book couldn't work, I put on the football suit anyway and then I made faces in the mirror and practiced looking tough. I also growled and made mean noises.

After a while I got tired of growling at myself in the mirror so I took off the football stuff and put it back in my closet. While I was putting it in my closet I remembered my idea to hide in Sally's closet. It seemed like tonight might be a good time to do it because if I got killed tomorrow at football practice then I would have spent my whole life never seeing a live naked lady. Besides, I had run out of things to do.

I went to Sally's bedroom and stood in the mid-

64

dle of the room for a few minutes. Sally's room is pretty nice. It used to be pink but she got sick of it being pink last year because she said it looked too babyish and so she painted it bright orange. She has this huge bulletin board with programs from all the school musicals and a lot of pictures and some dead flowers stuck to it. She also has pictures of no-neck Bozo Blakely all over the place.

I went in the closet and I tripped over some shoes on the floor and fell back into the clothes. I had never been in Sally's closet before, although I had looked in her drawers once a long time ago to see what a girl's underwear is like. But this was the first time I had been in her closet, and it was a lot smaller and a lot more jammed up with stuff than I thought it would be.

I got behind the clothes and then I pulled some dresses apart. One dress had some ruffles and a belt like a rope or something and I kept getting my hand all tangled up. When I finally got my hand untangled, I reached through the dresses and pulled the door shut all but just a crack. Then I peeked out and I could see pretty good right into the room over near the dresser which I hoped was where Sally would get undressed.

I looked at my Mickey Mouse watch which glows in the dark and it was almost nine o'clock. I had heard Sally say that she'd be home at nine and I hoped she wouldn't be late because it was getting very stuffy in that closet.

It seemed like about five million years that I was stuck in that closet instead of five minutes, but I finally heard the front door slam and Sally coming up the stairs. She was humming. Sally's always humming or singing. I thought she'd come into her room but she didn't because I heard a door close and then in a little while I heard the toilet flush and then the water running so I knew she was in the bathroom.

It seemed like forever, but she finally came into her room.

The first thing she did was turn on the lights, and then she went to the table by her bed and turned on her radio. I was glad about that because my heart was pounding real loud because I was beginning to get very nervous, and I was also afraid she could hear me breathing or something.

The next thing she did was to take off her shoes. I leaned close to the crack so I could see and what I saw was Sally walking over toward the closet and before I knew it she was opening the door.

"*Boo!*" I yelled real loud and jumped out.

"*Eeeek! Norman, you little creep! What are you doing?*"

I ran out of Sally's room yelling, "Just practicing for Halloween. Ha-ha-ha. Scared you, didn't I?" Then I ran in my room and Sally came right after me.

She stomped into my room. "Norman, that's not a bit funny—you are so weird! I don't know what's wrong with you. Don't ever do that again, and I'm telling Mom." Then Sally slammed the door and stomped out in her bare feet which was the only bare stuff I got to see.

I sure hoped Sally believed what I said about Halloween because I sure didn't want her to think I was some kind of pervert or something. I also hoped she wouldn't tell Mom.

I started feeling awful. Nothing was working out. The after-school project had seemed like a big success until Dad got mad and I ended up having to talk to Mrs. Beekin and show her the lamp, and the *Winning Through Intimidation* book that said I could learn to deal from a position of strength just ended up to be about the real-estate business, and now I was probably going to be in trouble for scaring Sally and I didn't even get to see anything. Now, besides having a G-rated life, my whole life seemed to be a mess.

Just as I thought, when Mom and Dad came home Sally told Mom about me being in her closet. I was fooling around in my room with the model I had bought at the garage sale when Mom came in my room.

"Norman, I want to talk to you."

"Just a minute, Mom, I have to go to the bathroom." I got up from the floor where I had the model stuff spread out all over and I ran out of the room.

I went into the bathroom, locked the door, and turned the water on, and then for no reason I started to cry. I was just in there sitting on the john with the seat down and all, and the water running and crying like a real jerk. I must have been in there for a long time because finally Mom came and knocked on the door.

"Norman? Are you all right?"

"Yeah."

"Are you sure?"

"Yeah."

"Well, I'll be waiting for you in your room when you're done in there."

I didn't say anything.

"Norman?"

"Yeah."

"Did you hear me?"

"Yeah." I quit sitting on the john and went to the sink and splashed cold water on my face. Then I blew my nose. I felt like an idiot about crying like that but it just seemed to happen and sometimes a person can't help it.

I unlocked the bathroom door and went back to my room. Mom was waiting in there. She was sitting on my bed.

"Norman," Mom said in this serious voice, "Sally says you really scared her tonight."

"It was just a joke," I said, and I looked down at the floor. It was hard to look at Mom.

"Norman, jokes like that aren't funny."

"I'm sorry, Mom."

"Norman, I want you to apologize to Sally and promise me you'll never do that again."

"Okay." I kind of shuffled my feet around. I wished Mom would leave, and I was afraid I might start crying again because my throat still had this lump in it.

"Norman, are you sure you're all right?" Mom looked down at me, and I guess you could say I didn't exactly have the happiest face in the whole world.

"Yeah. I mean . . . well, no, not exactly."

Mom put her arm around me. "What's wrong, honey?"

68

"Nothing, I guess—except, well . . ." Finally I just blurted out, "Football." And then Mom wiped this tear off my face and I felt like a jerk again and I just wished I hadn't said anything. But then she hugged me and I guess that was okay.

"You don't want to be on the team?"

"No. I know I won't be any good. I'm never going to be like him."

"It's so important to Dad, Norman." Mom sounded sad.

"I know. He got me his old number and everything."

"I feel kind of in the middle, honey," Mom said, and she sounded even more sad.

"You do?"

"Yes. Playing football was probably the most exciting time of Dad's life and he wants so much for you to love it. Actually, it's even more than that. I think he wants it to be almost like he's out there playing again through you."

"But how are you in the middle, Mom? Do you want me to be on the team?"

"Well, I'm in the middle because I love both of you and I want to see both of you happy. And I guess I've known all along that you're just doing it for him."

"But, Mom—do you want me to be on the team?"

Mom was quiet for a long time and I noticed she had started to cry.

"Now I guess it's my turn." She blew her nose. Finally she said softly, "It's not important to me that you be on the team, Norman," and she wiped her eyes.

"It's okay, Mom," I said, and I patted her hand.

It's hard to know what to do when your mother's crying.

Then Mom hugged me again and she told me she loved me and then she left. On her way out of my room she reminded me to apologize to Sally and she sounded sadder than before even.

I went to Sally's room and she was on the phone with Bozo Blakely. I stood in the door and Sally said, "Just a minute, John," and covered up the phone receiver.

"What d'ya want, Norman?"

"I'm sorry I scared you, Sally."

"Okay. Just don't ever do that again."

"Okay."

"Norman, what's wrong with you, anyway?"

"Nothing." I left Sally's room and went back to my room. "Nothing's wrong," I said to myself. "Just my whole life."

6

I was still feeling terrible Monday morning, but then a great thing happened at the bus stop, and the great thing was that Carrie Koski was there. I hadn't realized that she was going to be taking the same bus and all.

"Hi, Norman." Carrie smiled and she seemed real glad to see me. She was standing with a bunch of people, but no one was talking to her. They were all just talking to each other.

"Hi, Carrie. I didn't know you'd be taking this bus."

"Well, I wasn't sure it was the right one until you came."

"Do you know what class you're gonna be in yet?"

"No, I'm supposed to go to the office when I get to the school and then they'll tell me what class I'm

71

in. Would you show me where the office is when we get there?"

"Sure." I liked that idea very much. "I can wait with you in the office and then show you to your class if you want, too."

"But what if you're late?"

"I don't care." And that was the truth, too. I didn't care one bit if I was late. All that would happen anyway would be that Sleazy would yell at me.

This morning Carrie had on this T-shirt and it said, "The Right Side of the Brain Controls the Left Side of the Body. This Means Left-handed People Are the Only Ones in Their Right Minds." I read the shirt but then I felt kind of embarrassed looking at the shirt if you know what I mean. But it's hard not to stare at girls' shirts sometimes and just look at their faces.

"You must be left-handed," I said, and I quit looking at the shirt.

"Yeah. I got this T-shirt at a garage sale for fifty cents."

"Did you get it at one of those you went to on Sunday?"

"No, a different one a few weeks ago."

Just then P.W. came running up and he got to the bus stop just as the bus was pulling up.

"P.W., this is Carrie," I said. "She's new."

They said "Hi" and we all got in the bus and sat on one of the seats where you can fit three people. P.W. got in first, then Carrie, then me so she was in the middle. We were kind of squished but I didn't mind being squished next to Carrie Koski and she smelled good too, I noticed.

"Is P.W. your real name?" Carrie asked.

"No, my real name's Peter Wilcox—but everyone calls me P.W. 'cause I got some pussy willows stuck up my nose in second grade."

"Yeah, and he had to go to the emergency room at Harborview Hospital to get 'em out," I told Carrie.

"One time I stuck Puffed Wheat cereal up my nose," Carrie said, "but I got it out."

"Where'd ya move here from?" P.W. asked.

"The Shorewood Apartments."

"Is that in Seattle?" I asked Carrie, because I wanted to stay in the conversation and not just have P.W. talk to her.

"No, it's on Mercer Island."

Then old McCabe started yelling at everyone to shut up like he always does even though I didn't think the bus was that noisy.

When we got to school, I walked Carrie to the office and P.W. hung around on the playground until it was time for the bell. A lot of people from our class were messing around on the playground, and I liked walking in the school with Carrie Koski and having it just be me taking her to the office.

In the office, Mrs. Marcelli, the secretary, asked if she could help us and Carrie told Mrs. Marcelli her name and that she was new and stuff.

"Oh, yes, Carrie. I've talked to your mother on the phone and we already have your records from your old school. Welcome to Evergreen Elementary." Then Mrs. Marcelli went to her desk and looked at some papers.

"I'll just check and see what class assignment has been made for you." Then Mrs. Marcelli noticed me standing there. "Norman, is there any-thing I can help you with?"

"I'm waiting for Carrie," I told Mrs. Marcelli. "I can show her where her room is if you want."

"That would be very nice, Norman, thank you."

While we were waiting for Mrs. Marcelli to look up about Carrie's class the first bell rang. Everyone came piling in the school and we could hear the principal, Mr. Sanchez, out in the hall yelling at everyone to keep their voices down and not to run in the halls. Then Mrs. Marcelli had to answer the phone and we waited until she got off. By the time she got off the phone, the second bell had already rung and I knew Sleazy would be calling the roll.

"Carrie," Mrs. Marcelli said, "you'll be in Ms. Claremont's sixth-grade class. That's in room 220, and be sure to give this to Ms. Claremont." She handed Carrie a slip of paper.

"Mrs. Marcelli," I asked, "do you think I could have a late excuse?"

"Of course, Norman." Mrs. Marcelli took out a pink excuse form and wrote in the time and signed it.

Carrie and I left the office and walked down the hall and up the stairs to where room 220 was. I liked walking around the empty halls with Carrie and also having an excuse from the office. I usually don't get picked to do special jobs for the office where you get an excuse.

"I wish you had gotten assigned to my class, Carrie."

"You mean you don't have Ms. Claremont?" She sounded worried.

"No. I'm in the other sixth-grade class. I'm in Slezak's.

"Oh. That's too bad."

"Yeah."

We got to room 220 and stood outside the door for a minute.

"I'm kind of afraid to go in there," Carrie said.

"It'll be all right. I'll see you at lunch."

"Okay." Carrie put her hand on the doorknob and looked back at me. "Norman?"

"Yeah?"

"Thanks."

"Sure," I said and I watched as she went in. I walked down the hall to 235, which is my room, and I felt really great. I stopped at the drinking fountain and got a drink of water. I squirted the drinking fountain on and off a few times just for the fun of it. Then I went into my room and walked right up to Mr. Slezak and handed him the excuse. Sleazy said, "Fine," and I got in my seat.

Finally lunch came and I went down to the lunchroom and sat at the table where I usually sit with P.W., Robbie Miller, Matt Sato, Eric Silverman and Henry Williams. Everyone brought their lunch except for Robbie who forgot his. He had to borrow lunch money from the office and he had to go through the lunch line and get the brown gooey stew which looked disgusting and kept getting stuck in his braces. The only good stuff he got was a cinnamon roll and everyone wanted a bite of that, especially Eric Silverman who almost ate the whole thing.

I looked around the lunchroom while we were

passing Robbie's cinnamon roll around and I saw Carrie over in the corner. She was sitting at this table by herself and she seemed real alone. I wanted to go over there and sit with her, but one thing about Evergreen Elementary is that guys never eat lunch with girls. If I left our table and went over there I knew everyone, especially Eric Silverman, would make a big deal about it and it would be very embarrassing. I thought maybe I could eat real slow or maybe go to the bathroom and then come back and hope that by then the guys would have gone out on the playground to mess around. But that plan might not be too good, 'cause then Carrie might be gone too.

I kept thinking about this a lot, and then, I don't know, I guess I just finally decided that if I could pull a dead rat out of the gutter with my bare hands that I could walk across the whole lunchroom in front of the guys and everybody and sit with Carrie Koski so she could have some company.

I picked up my tray and left the table. It seemed like about ten miles across the lunchroom to where Carrie was sitting.

"Where ya going, Schnurman?" Eric Silverman asked.

"Gotta talk to someone," I mumbled, hoping they wouldn't pay attention. But as I got over near Carrie's table in the corner, Eric Silverman started yelling, "Where's Norman Nurdman?" so I turned around and gave him the finger. Then I sat down at Carrie's table.

"Hi, Norman!" Carrie smiled. "I'm glad you came over."

"How was your morning in Claremont's room?"

"Okay, I guess. But she has me sitting between two guys and I haven't gotten to talk to any of the girls yet." Carrie looked over at a table of girls near the door of the lunchroom. "Those girls are all in my class but no one asked me to sit with them and I didn't want to just barge in. You feel like a jerk if you go up to people and just barge in."

"Yeah, I know what you mean."

"I don't like being new."

"Yeah. How come you had to move?"

"Well, we'd been looking for a house in the city for a long time because my Mom got transferred to an office downtown and she got tired of driving across the bridge."

"Yeah. The bridge is always getting stuck."

Carrie and I kept talking and she told me that her Mom worked for the telephone company, she was an engineer or something like that, and she said her grandfather doesn't work anymore since he retired from being a crab fisherman in Alaska, but he volunteers at the zoo. Carrie said he likes birds a lot so he hangs out around the special birdhouse they have in the zoo. I guess Mr. Koski goes to the aviary three mornings a week. Carrie was telling me all about Mr. Koski hanging out at the birdhouse at the zoo when I looked out the window and saw all the guys from my lunch table in this tree. They were hanging from the branches and peeking in at me and Carrie, waving their arms around, making stupid kissing faces and acting like a bunch of perverts.

"Just a second, Carrie," I said, and I got up from the table and stood at the window with my back to her so she couldn't see me giving those guys the finger again.

"What did you do, Norman?" Carrie asked as I sat back down at the table.

"Oh, just giving those guys I know out there a secret wave we have."

"Oh."

Then the bell rang and Carrie and I walked out of the lunchroom together.

"Norman, are you going to any garage sales this weekend?"

"Yeah, I go every weekend."

"So do we. Why don't you go with me and Gramps. We could meet at my house and then go from there."

"Great. Where do you live?"

Carrie looked kind of blank. Then she laughed because I think she was embarrassed.

"Do you believe that!" Carrie started giggling. "I forgot my house number!"

I laughed too. "Well, it's new and all . . ."

"Yeah," Carrie laughed. "But here's what—if you want to, on your way home from school I could show you what house it is."

"Great!" I said—and then I remembered. "Oh . . . I mean, no—I can't."

"Oh."

"I have football practice."

"Oh." Then the lunch bell rang. "Well—'bye, Norman. See you later," Carrie said, and I watched her walk down the hall. After school I wished I was over at Carrie's house seeing where she lived instead of doing what I was doing, which was putting on the football suit and waiting for my Dad to come pick me up.

When I got home I was hungry so I thought I would eat a little snack. I made three peanut-butter-and-jelly sandwiches and had two glasses of milk. I am also the kind of person who eats when they are nervous and that's what I was—nervous. I also thought it would be a good idea to eat so it might make me fatter. This is because the football league is divided into three divisions. There is the midget division and to be in that you have to be seven or eight years old and in the backfield and not weigh more than seventy-five pounds. Then there is the junior division for people nine and ten and they can't weigh more than ninety-five pounds. The Bears are in the intermediate division which is for guys eleven and twelve and they can't weigh more than one hundred and fifteen pounds. But they have different weight rules for the people in the backfield. Those are the ones who run with the ball and they can't weigh more than one hundred and five pounds. I weigh ninety-nine pounds and I wished I could be in the midget division even though those guys are only seven and eight. But then I kind of hoped that if I got too fat I wouldn't have to be in the backfield and have to run with the ball and have everyone jump on top of me. Maybe I could play on the line and just sort of hide out in there.

I was looking over the playbook and the rules and stuff while I was waiting for Dad to come. In the rulebook I noticed that there was this rule that said that in the intermediate division the use of mouth guards was mandatory. The rule said that all players had to wear a mouth guard or else they would be in violation of the rules. This really made me nervous. It also made me wish even more that I was in the midget division because when you're seven or eight you don't have all your permanent teeth in anyway, so if you get them knocked out you can just grow some more teeth. But I have all my permanent teeth so if I get some knocked out, I'll have to get false teeth. I am too young to have false teeth.

I was picturing me having to go to junior high with these false teeth and a tube of Polident sticking out of my back pocket when I heard the car in the driveway. Dad was home.

He came up the stairs and into my room. "Great. Glad to see you're all ready, Norman. I'll change into my sweats and we can go in just a few minutes."

I looked at the playbook some more while Dad changed, and then he was ready. He was wearing his old Husky warm-ups and he even had a whistle around his neck.

As Dad drove me to the Rainier playfield, I was thinking back over my life trying to remember if I had ever had any victories. The only one I could think of wasn't even a first-place finish—but it was coming in second and that was in the peeing contest we used to have in the third grade. During lunch some of the guys in my class would all go in the boys' bathroom together and we'd all stand back and pee and see who could get the farthest away and still hit the thing. But I didn't think coming in second in the third-grade peeing contest really counted as an athletic achievement.

I was thinking about this when Dad said, "It's a great day for football, isn't it, Norman? You know, on a day like this when the sky is clear and blue and the air is crisp and the leaves are turning—well, it's just a great football day." He rolled down the window and took a deep breath. "Yep, there's just something about that special smell in the air— brings back such great memories for me: the band playing, the roar of the crowd." Dad looked over at me and put his arm around me. "It's good to be going to a football field on a day like this with you, Norman."

7

We got to the Rainier playfield and got out of the car. Dad went around to the trunk and opened it. He took out a large chalk board and then slammed the trunk shut. I carried my helmet and Dad carried the chalk board and we walked across the park to the edge of the football field. The ground was wet and squishy because it had rained so much last week. There was a big puddle near the field and I looked at it and kind of wished I could splash around in it and maybe make a few mud pies. I haven't done anything like that since first grade. But I followed Dad instead of screwing around in the puddle.

He set the chalk board up against a tree, and in a few minutes guys started to arrive at the field and come over to where we were waiting. I recognized a few guys from the other sixth-grade class, but a lot of the others I didn't know. But then a big guy came, and I knew him for sure, because it was Eric Silverman.

"Schnurman—what are you doing here?"

"My Dad's the coach."

"Oh, yeah, Mr. Pierce told us we'd be getting our new coach today. I didn't know you liked football."

"Yeah, well . . ." I wanted to tell Eric that I didn't, but Dad was looking at us. "I thought I'd give it a try," I said.

Pretty soon everyone was there. There were eighteen people in all. The rules say that's all you can have. The team was already full when Mr. Pierce left, but his son was on the team so that's how come there was an opening for me. I wish Mr. Pierce's son had decided to stay in Seattle and not move to Kansas with Mr. Pierce.

My Dad blew the whistle and got everyone to sit around in a semicircle on the ground around the tree where he had propped the chalk board.

"Well, as you all know, Mr. Pierce had to move, and today I'll be taking over as your new coach," my Dad said. "My name is Dave Schnurman and this is my son, Norman." Dad pointed to me. "He'll be taking Brad Pierce's place."

When Dad said that everyone looked at me and I got embarrassed. Then this one guy I didn't know raised his hand.

"Are you Mad Dog Dave Schnurman?" he asked my Dad.

Dad laughed. "Well, that's what they used to call me and I guess some people still do—but that was quite a bit before your time."

"I heard of you," the guy said, " 'cause my Dad talks about you."

"Yeah, mine too," a few other guys said, and they all seemed real impressed.

Then this guy turned to me. "You must really be good," he said.

I just shook my head, but everyone looked at me again.

"Now, it's going to take me a while to get to learn your names, but I'd like you to start now and go around the circle and each tell me your name and what position you've been playing."

Everyone did what my Dad said, and when it got to be Eric Silverman's turn, he said "quarterback" after his name.

"That figures," I thought to myself. Then it was my turn to do it. "Norman Schnurman, running back," I said.

"Tailback," my father corrected me. "Technically, anyone who carries the ball is called a running back, but in our formation your specific position is called tailback."

"Tailback," I said.

"All right. Now, the first thing I want to tell you is that I won't allow anyone to talk while I'm talking. If you want to learn to play football you have to concentrate and you can't do that if you're talking instead of listening to me." Then he glared at some guys who were whispering and they both shut up real quick.

"The second thing I want you to know is that I expect you to ask questions. I had a great teacher once who told me that if you don't learn something it's not because you are a poor student . . . that is, if you're really trying. It's because the teacher hasn't tried hard enough to find a way to get across to you what you're being taught. So it's my job as coach to explain things to you as many times and as many ways as I have to—until you get it. And it's your job, as students of this great game of football, to ask me questions and tell me if you don't understand."

I was surprised to hear my Dad say that stuff. He seemed kind of like a real teacher up there and all. But I wondered if he really meant that stuff because I always thought he thought it was my fault that I get C's.

Then he said that he would diagram three plays from our playbook on the chalk board. Then we would do wind sprints and then we would scrimmage. I was kind of hoping that when my Dad drew all the stuff on the board that people would ask so many questions that we would take up the whole practice and have to forget the wind sprint part and the scrimmage part. But no such luck.

After about fifteen minutes the sitting-around-the-chalk-board part of the practice was over and we all got up, put on our helmets and lined up on the goal line for the wind sprints.

"All right, men," Dad yelled, "now I want you all in a three-point stance."

I wasn't exactly sure what that was so I copied the guy next to me. I hunched over with my feet apart and leaned my right hand on the ground.

"Now, men, I'm going to say 'Ready . . . set . . .'

and then blow the whistle. When you hear the whistle, run as fast as you can up to the ten-yard line. Get in another three-point stance, we'll wait until everyone is lined up and then when you hear the whistle again, do the same thing and sprint to the twenty. We'll continue on up the field this way for eighty yards."

While I was hunched over in the three-point stance, I wondered why we were only supposed to do wind sprints for eighty yards, but then I remembered in Junior Football League the field is only supposed to be eighty yards long. I was also worrying if I would be the last one to get to the ten-yard line when I heard my Dad.

"Ready . . . set . . . *tweeeeeeet!*"

It was a lot harder to run fast wearing all that football crap than I expected, but I went as fast as I could. When I got to the ten-yard line, I got into another three-point stance and then I looked around. I wasn't the first one there, but I wasn't the last one either. I got there kind of in the middle.

"Ready . . . set . . . *tweeeeeeet!*"

I ran as fast as I could to the twenty, and I ended up in the middle again. We kept doing this thing all the way down the field until we got to the other twenty-yard line, and every time, I ended up in the middle. I felt real happy about this, but one thing I did not feel happy about was that I was beginning to feel kind of sick. I guess my stomach hurt from running like that because I just wasn't used to it.

"All right, men, that looked pretty good. There's just no better conditioning than wind sprints."

Then Dad turned to the guys who had come in

first every time. "Tyler, Silverman—that was good quickness."

I know this sounds stupid, but I was kind of jealous that he was saying nice stuff to those guys. I thought it was a big deal that I had ended up in the middle and not come in last.

"Now," Dad said to everyone, "I want the defense to put on the blue practice jerseys. Offense—stay as you are, and when the defense is ready, we'll scrimmage."

While the defense was putting on the shirts—I guess so Dad could tell them apart from us—he came over to the rest of us.

"Offense—I want you to use the three plays that we went over on the chalk board, 21 Dive, 37 Sweep and 33 Slant. Do you all know your assignments?"

Everybody said "Yeah" except me. I thought I knew, but I wasn't completely sure and I didn't want to say anything and sound like a jerk. I was trying to remember if I was supposed to carry the ball on 21 Dive or 37 Sweep. I felt more sure of what I was supposed to do on 33 Slant. On that one the quarterback fakes and pretends he's going to give the ball to the two back, the fullback, but then he hands it to me and I'm supposed to slant to the left and run through the three hole—between the guard and the tackle. I guess the hole is supposed to get there by the guys on the line who block the defense out of the way for me.

Dad went over to Eric Silverman. "Quarterback, I want you to call one of those plays in the huddle— it's your choice which one you want to run first."

Eric said "Okay" and then Dad carried the ball and put it down in the middle of the forty-yard line.

"We won't have a kickoff in the scrimmage, men. We'll start here with the first down for the white shirts." Dad walked over to the sideline and put the whistle in his mouth, and we got in the huddle.

It was hot and sweaty in that huddle with everyone all squished up and breathing on each other. We all looked at Eric.

"Slot left," Eric said, "33 Slant . . . on two." Everyone clapped and we ran up to the line of scrimmage. I was glad Eric had called that play first, because I knew my assignment.

"Tweeeeeeet!"

"Ready . . . set . . . hut one . . . hut two . . ." yelled Eric, then the ball was snapped. Eric pivoted around and faked like he was handing off the ball to Clarence Tyler. Then I slanted to the left and Eric shoved the ball in my stomach.

I doubled over, and I slanted all right—I ran on a slant right over to the sideline. I didn't lose the ball, but what I lost was the three peanut-butter sandwiches and the two glasses of milk. I threw up right there on the side of the field.

"Oh, yuk!" Silverman said. But Clarence Tyler was nice.

He came over to the sideline and asked me if I was okay.

Then my Dad came over.

He put his hand on my shoulder, "Norman—did you have a lot to eat before practice?"

"Yeah. I thought it would make me fatter."

"Well, you should never load up on food right before practice or a game. You can get sick that way."

"I noticed."

"Okay—now, do you still feel sick?"

"Kind of."

"Then I think you should sit out the rest of the practice."

"I don't want to throw up again here—I think I'll just walk home if that's okay with you."

"I'd drive you home, but—"

"No, it's okay, Dad. You stay with the team."

I walked over to the drinking fountain and cleaned up my face. Then I got my helmet. I left the field and walked home alone.

8

I walked pretty slowly on my way home. When I got by the park I was just kind of shuffling along, just kicking leaves and stuff, when I heard this voice behind me.

"Well, hello, Norman."

I turned around and it was Mr. Koski, Carrie's grandfather.

"Hi, Mr. Koski," I mumbled.

"That's a nice uniform you got there, Norman. I didn't know you were a football player."

"It's got barf on it."

"What?"

"It's got barf on it—my uniform. I threw up at practice and I'm not a football player." I just blurted that out and then I started kicking some leaves.

"Oh." Mr. Koski didn't say anything for a few

minutes and we just stood there while I kicked leaves. Then he asked me how my stomach felt.

"Still a little shaky—but not too bad."

"Is anyone home at your house?"

"No."

"I'll tell you what, Norman. Why don't you go home, change out of your uniform and then come on over to our house. I'll fix you my special blend of tea. Lars Koski's tea can fix anything. I used it for years on my boat up in Alaska, and I guarantee Koski's tea cured flu, seasickness, just the shakes, anything. You name it—I cured it."

I looked up at Mr. Koski and I thought that going over to his house wouldn't be any worse than just being home alone and feeling like a jerk. Besides, Carrie might be there, so I said, "Okay."

"It's on Plum Street, the second from the corner on the right—number 3250."

"Okay."

When I got home I put my football suit in the washing machine and went up to my room. I got out the playbook and tried to study it for a few minutes before I got ready to go to Mr. Koski's house.

I was dreading the game Saturday. I knew Dad would put me in for some of it because the league rules say that every guy on the team has to be in every game—even if it's just for a little while. I looked at that playbook and so far the only play I was sure of was 33 Slant and that had been a disaster. And it seemed like the only thing I had learned for sure was not to eat a bunch of stuff before football.

I went down to the basement and got my football stuff out of the washing machine. Before I put it in the dryer, I smelled it and it didn't smell like barf anymore.

Then I got my bike out of the garage and I rode over to Plum Street. The Koskis' house was nice. It was white with dark blue shutters and it had a huge maple tree in the front yard. Mr. Koski let me in and as I followed him in the house, I kind of worried what Carrie would think since I had told her that I couldn't come and see where she lived today because of football practice.

Mr. Koski and I went in the kitchen and I sat down at the kitchen table while he rummaged around in the cupboards.

"Is Carrie home?" I asked.

"She was here, but a neighbor called and asked if Carrie could come over and baby-sit for her while she went to the store—so Carrie's next door now."

Mr. Koski got an old tin down out of the cupboard and put it on the stove. Then he got the teakettle and went to the sink and filled it with water. He got two cups out of the cupboard and put them on the kitchen table and put the teakettle on the stove and turned it on.

"So it was pretty rough today, huh, Norman?" Mr. Koski said as he scooped out the tea from the tin and dumped it in the bottom of the teapot.

"Uh-huh. I felt like a real jerk in front of all the guys."

Mr. Koski took his pipe out of his shirt pocket and lit it and chewed on it for a while. "You know, Norman, a great lady named Eleanor Roosevelt once said that no one can make you feel inferior without your consent. I do believe that lady was right."

Then the teakettle started whistling and Mr. Koski got up from the table, turned it off, and poured the boiling water in the teapot. While he was fixing the tea, I thought about what he said. I wasn't exactly sure what it meant, but I thought it sounded pretty good.

Mr. Koski held a tea strainer over our cups and poured us each a cup of the tea. "You want some lemon? Or some sugar and cream?" he asked.

"Sugar'd be good."

Mr. Koski got up and got me a spoon and brought over the sugar bowl. I took a couple of spoonfuls and stirred it around in the tea. My stomach seemed to feel better already and I hadn't even tasted the stuff yet. It must have been good for you just to smell it.

We sat there and didn't say anything for a while and just sipped our tea.

"You know, Mr. Koski—I just don't think I'm ever going to make it," I said, kind of quiet.

"Make what?"

"Be a football player, like my Dad. My Dad was Mad Dog Dave Schnurman, he held the rushing record for the Huskies for fifteen years. He gave me his old number and I'm supposed to be a tailback, like him. And now he's the coach of the Bears football team and he says I gotta be on the Bears. I'm no good at football, in fact I don't even like it. All I've done so far is just run into chairs and throw up and we have our first game on Saturday."

"That certainly is a problem." Mr. Koski seemed real understanding. "My father had a cannery in Alaska. He always wanted me to be in the cannery business, but I loved the sea. I tried the cannery business for a while but I always wanted to be out on the boats." Mr. Koski scratched his head. "My father never could understand that. Yep. That's a tough one all right. I don't suppose there's anything in this world that a boy wants more than his father's approval."

Mr. Koski sipped his tea. "Well, Norman, maybe the Lord didn't intend for you to be a football player, but there sure are other things you can do. Why, a young man as bright as you—I bet you do real well in school."

"Nope. I get C's."

"That's all I got. But nothing wrong with that. Abraham Lincoln said that common people are the best in the world and that's the reason the Lord makes so many of them."

"I wish my Dad thought that."

"Besides that, Norman, you never can tell what'll happen to a person just from how they're doing in school. Albert Einstein didn't even learn to talk for years, and then in school his headmaster told his father that it didn't matter what profession Einstein was interested in because he'd never make a success at anything. They also say he dropped out of school when he was sixteen."

"Really?"

"That's what they say. Now, I'm not tellin' you to drop out of school. Don't get me wrong—but there are a lot of men who went on to make their mark in the world who didn't do well in school. I used to like to collect information on those kind of guys."

"Yeah—like who?"

"Well, let's see. Winston Churchill didn't have much education. President Eisenhower was a real good C fellow and Thomas Edison only went to school for three months. He started work as a newsboy on the Grand Trunk Railway when he was twelve." Mr. Koski chewed on his pipe and thought for a few minutes. "But actually, I'm not sure how much that information about famous people helps."

"Yeah, I know what you mean." I sipped on my tea. It sure was good. I was starting to feel better. Mr. Koski sure was right about that tea.

"More tea, Norman?"

"Sure. Thanks."

Mr. Koski went to the stove and got the teapot and filled our cups again.

"Mr. Koski? How do you know all that stuff—about all those famous people and stuff?"

"Well, I like to read a lot and especially I did a lot of reading when we were out at sea. Although I must say that as far as famous people go—I always thought folks ought to try to be superstars at being decent human beings. But I guess I'd say I learned more about human nature out at sea than I think I ever did anyplace else."

"About human nature?"

"Yep, Norman, and especially about what it means to be a man." Mr. Koski sipped on his tea and puffed his pipe some more. "You see, this problem you've got with your father and the foot-

95

ball, the way I figure it—it's a little bit about figuring out just how to be a man—'cause if a boy has a big, strong, aggressive guy for a father and if the boy's not exactly like that, sometimes he wonders if he'll ever grow up to be a real man if he's not like his Dad."

"I guess so."

"Now, if you've got the time, I'll tell you a story about being big and strong and tough."

"Sure, Mr. Koski."

"You're real sure, now? Because Carrie's always gettin' after me for talkin' to folks too much and tellin' too many old stories."

"I'd like to hear, Mr. Koski."

"Well, now, you just wait a minute and I'll go get one of the logs from when I captained my fishing boat up in Alaska." Mr. Koski seemed real happy.

He explained to me that the log is a book where the captain would write down about everything that happened each day when they were out to sea. When he came back with the log it had started to rain and Mr. Koski asked me if I'd like to help him make a fire.

"There's a fireplace in the den and we could take our tea in there if you'd like."

I said "Sure" and I followed Mr. Koski to the den.

"You like to make fires, Norman?"

"I like to a lot."

"Well, have at it. There's the stuff," he said, pointing at a cardboard box which was full of old newspapers, kindling and logs. Then he sat back in his rocking chair and lit his pipe and watched while I made the fire.

I crumpled up all the papers and then I put the kindling on top. I put the logs on top of that and then I got a match from Mr. Koski and lit it. The paper caught and then the kindling. The twigs started to crackle and then pretty soon the logs were burning.

"You make a fine fire, Norm," Mr. Koski said. "More tea?"

"Thanks. It's good, I feel a lot better."

Mr. Koski had brought the teapot in the den and poured us each another cup. "Yep, Koski's tea'll do it every time."

I sat down by the fire and Mr. Koski rocked in his chair. He held the log on his lap. It was an old leather book and it looked kind of dusty. Mr. Koski blew the dust off and slowly turned the pages.

"I don't know how much you know about a crab boat, Norm—but I had one of the best around. Yes siree, the *North Star* was hard to beat. She was ninety-six feet long, the wheelhouse was on top and the captain's bunk next to it. The deck was underneath that and that's where we had the hydraulic boom to which we attached the crab pots. Now, crab pot may sound like something small, but those things are six feet by six feet by four feet, and each one weighs upwards near two hundred pounds." Mr. Koski sipped on his tea.

"Underneath the deck were the bunks. The *North Star* had one bunk room with two bunks and another with four, and of course a head—that's the toilet. Down underneath the bunks was the engine room. The *North Star*, well—she was one of the finest boats to fish the waters of Alaska. I sure did

hate to sell her"—Mr. Koski puffed on his pipe—
"but it was time."

I poked the fire. It was burning real good.

"I always had a five-man crew," Mr. Koski said as
he turned the pages of the log. "There was me, the
cook—who didn't just cook. Old Jake was always
right up there with the rest of the crew when it
came time to bring up the pots. And we had an
engineer, who maintained the engines and the
equipment, and then we had two deckhands.

"One of my deckhands broke his foot. A two-
hundred-pound crab pot had landed on it and I tell
you—there's a lot of things Koski's tea can fix, but
it can't fix a broken foot. We had to head back to
our port at Naknek, in Bristol Bay. We had been
four miles offshore in the Bering Sea near Nelson
Lagoon on the north side of the Alaska Peninsula,
five hundred fifty miles southwest of Anchorage,
when it happened." Mr. Koski looked at his log and
then took another sip of his tea.

"I had to get a new deckhand as quick as I could.
All my pots were on the bottom of the ocean and I
knew with a man short we might not be able to get
'em all. I went into Naknek and found a guy there
that was looking to sign on with a crab boat. He
had been up riggin' the pipeline for the oil and I
guess had had enough of that and thought he'd try
his hand at fishin'. He was a great big guy and as
mean as they come. Seemed like he was always in
the bar and in one fight after the other. That fella
sure did like to fight. I usually don't take that kind
on my crew, but you see, Norm, I was desperate. So
I signed him up. Jack Johnson was his name. That

fella was big, strong and tough—and he was big everywhere—all his bodily parts, too."

I kind of giggled and kept poking at the fire.

"Yep, we sure thought he was some man. So I signed him up. The fellas on the crew, well, they didn't call him Jack Johnson for long. Nope, they gave him a nickname real quick. They called Jack Johnson 'Moby Dick'—after the killer whale, of course." Mr. Koski winked.

Then he got up and poured himself some more tea and sat in the rocking chair again and turned the pages of the log.

"We went back out into Nelson Lagoon to pick up our pots and a storm brewed up. Man, did she brew up. Norm, it was the worst one I'd seen in all my years of fishing the Bering Sea. I had to make a decision then—whether to leave those pots and head back or to get the crabs and my equipment before it got too late.

"Well, I decided to go for it. We had at least two hundred pots out—each string had twenty pots and our buoys were even beginning to break off. You see, each pot is attached to a buoy, Norm, and after you lower 'em down to the bottom you go back and pick 'em all up. You swing the pots over the deck, and then as fast as you can all the deckhands throw the keepers into the hatch, down into the holding tank. The females and the little 'uns you throw back into the sea. A good catch can be worth hundreds of thousands of dollars, and I was determined to beat that storm. Well, the *North Star*—she was pitching and rolling and I called for all hands on deck to start bringing up the pots. They all showed, too, just working fast and furious. All except for Moby Dick. He was nowhere to be seen. I called out his name but I didn't think I could be heard—that wind was howling so loud—so I looked below deck. Moby Dick wasn't in the bunk room and I got an awful start. I worried he'd been washed overboard. But I went down to the engine room and that's where I found him. Yep—there he was, Moby Dick, biggest, meanest son of a gun that ever signed on a crab boat, all hunched over in the corner of the engine room just a-shakin' like a leaf."

"What happened, Mr. Koski?"

"Well, I didn't say anything to Moby Dick. I just went back up on deck and took over the wheel. We lost half our pots that day 'cause I knew I finally had to turn back. When we got back to Naknek, back on Bristol Bay, Jack Johnson left the *North Star* and was never seen again. That night when the crew was gettin' drunk in town, I thought it all over and I wrote down my thoughts in the log." Mr. Koski handed the log to me.

The log smelled like fish and the paper was thin and wrinkly. I looked down at what Mr. Koski had written, and it went like this:

1. One thing about being a man is that it doesn't matter how big you are, or your bodily parts, or how strong or tough you are.
2. Once you know that there isn't much else to know.
3. Except it's important to be good to the other fella and try to do your share.

Underneath that I noticed it was signed "Lars Koski." I looked up at Mr. Koski after I read what he had written in his log. "Here, Mr. Koski," I said, handing it to him. "I think that's real good stuff you wrote down."

It was starting to get dark, but the rain had stopped. I knew I had better be going home or else my Mom would worry and she was probably home from work by now. I knew Dad would be getting back from the football practice soon, too.

Mr. Koski walked me to the door and asked me if I'd like to go with him and Carrie to the garage sales this weekend. I sure wanted to and we agreed for me to come over after the football game on Saturday.

On the way home, I thought about Mr. Koski. I like him a lot. I don't think he talks too much.

9

When I got home, Mom was there and she had already started dinner.

"Norman, we're just having soup and sandwiches tonight. We have to leave at six-thirty to get Sally out to school. Tonight's the night." Mom seemed real excited. "The night for *Annie Get Your Gun*—don't you remember?"

"Oh, yeah." Actually, I had forgotten, I had been thinking so much about all the football stuff happening today.

"We'll go as soon as we finish dinner. Norman, how was football practice? Dad didn't say much about it. He's up in the shower." She sounded a little worried.

"It was okay—except I threw up."

"Are you all right?" Mom came over and felt my head.

"I'm fine. I just ate a bunch of junk before the practice, and Dad said not to do that again. I'll go get changed."

"Okay. Dinner will be ready soon."

I went up to my room and started to get changed. I was glad that tonight was Sally's deal because everyone would probably be all involved in that and not think too much about football practice—which had been a disaster as far as I was concerned. And I didn't want to tell Mom too much about it since she already was feeling stuck in the middle and stuff.

I heard Dad get out of the shower and I went in the bathroom so I could take a shower too before we went. Dad came out of the shower with a towel wrapped around his waist.

"How are you feeling, Norman?"

"Better. I'm okay, I guess."

"Good. With today and one more practice on Thursday, I'm sure the game Saturday will be a lot better and especially if you don't eat beforehand." Dad rumpled my hair on the way out of the bathroom. He seemed real happy. He was whistling the old Huskies' fight song.

I got in the shower. I stayed in there a long time. I like to fool around in the shower.

Sally's musical was a big success. I sat between Mom and Dad, and Bozo Blakely was there too. He sat next to Dad. They talked about football during the intermission.

At the end of the show everyone clapped and cheered and Sally took what I think was about three hundred bows. I have to say, she was great. I was proud of her.

On the way home in the car I decided to tell her so, too.

"You were great, Sally," I said.

Sally looked at me kind of funny; she seemed surprised.

"Thanks, Norman."

When we got back from *Annie Get Your Gun* I went right to bed because it was late, but I couldn't get to sleep right away. I was excited about Saturday. Not the football game, which I was dreading, but getting to be with Carrie and Mr. Koski. I even kind of wished that sometime I might get to do something all alone with Carrie. Even though I sure liked Mr. Koski, it would also be good to go somewhere alone with Carrie—like the movies, or maybe to Seattle Center and go on the rides. I was thinking about this so much that I had a hard time getting to sleep. I kept imagining me, Norman Schnurman, taking Carrie somewhere, like on a date sort of.

I got nervous thinking about this. I wondered what we would talk about, I thought it would probably be necessary for me to be funny and say things to make her laugh. So I started to think up jokes I could say to her. I don't know very many jokes, but I finally remembered this joke and I got up and put the light on.

I got a piece of paper and a pencil and decided that I should write down the joke and practice it, just in case I ever did get up the nerve to go somewhere alone with Carrie Koski like on a date. The joke went like this:

I would say, "What did one frog say to the other?"

Then Carrie would say, "I don't know. What?"

"Time's sure fun when you're having flies."

I sat in bed in my pajamas trying to think of more jokes, but I couldn't think of any more right away. Then I had to go to the bathroom. When I got back, I remembered another joke and so I wrote it down. The joke is supposed to happen if Carrie has to go to the bathroom if we're at the movies, or Seattle Center or wherever we are. I walk her to the bathroom and then right before she goes into the ladies' room I say, "Mention my name and you'll get a good seat."

I wrote down "bathroom joke" under the frog joke on the paper. I tried to think of some more jokes, but those were the only ones I could remember.

I turned out the light, but then I sat up in bed and pretended that I was at the movies sitting next to Carrie. Then I pretended that we were at Seattle Center on the rides, like the Ferris wheel. I would sure like to put my arm around her, but I couldn't figure out how to do that. I propped up my pillow next to me and practiced it. Finally I decided that the most sensible way to get my arm around her would be to put my arms behind my head, then I would do this loud fake sneeze and then my arm would fly out around the pillow. I was doing it for the fourth time when I heard a knock on my door.

"Norman?" Mom opened the door. "Are you all right? It sounds like you're getting a cold."

"No, Mom, I'm fine. Something just got in my nose, I guess."

Mom came over and felt my head. Then she kissed me. "Good night, honey, sleep well."

After Mom left, I decided not to practice anymore and I went to sleep. But right before I went to sleep I wondered how I'd ever get up the nerve to ask Carrie to go somewhere with me. The last thing I remember thinking was that maybe I could ask her when I saw her Saturday after the game.

It seemed like Saturday would never come, but it finally did. I studied the playbook all week and I think I finally learned all the plays. Dad would quiz me on them after dinner and I would tell him my assignment for each play. He seemed happy that I was learning them so well. But talking about football is sure not the same thing as playing it and in some ways I hoped the game would get canceled or something.

But it didn't. We were playing the Giants from West Seattle and when we got to the field I could see why they were called the Giants. Those guys sure seemed huge to me. They looked mean, too. There were a lot of parents standing on the sidelines and the referee came and he had on a real striped referee suit. My stomach felt shaky even though I had been careful not to eat a whole mess of stuff.

The Giants won the coin toss and they chose to receive. I was glad about that because our defense would have to get out there first and I wouldn't have to go in for a while.

But either the Giants' offense was crummy or our defense was real good, because within no time at all the Giants had used up all their downs and they had only gone a few yards. They were getting ready to punt on their next play and Dad sent in the offense.

"Go get 'em, men," Dad yelled while he paced up and down the sideline.

In the huddle, Eric Silverman called the play, "Slot left . . . 21 Dive . . . on three."

I was glad he called that one because Clarence Tyler is supposed to carry the ball and not me. All I have to do is delay one count after the snap and then pretend like I have the ball after Eric fakes to me. Then I run off to the side.

We lined up and Eric called out, "Ready . . . set . . . hut one . . . hut two . . . hut three . . ."

I waited one count after the snap and pretended that I had the ball after Eric faked to me. Then I ran off to the side. It didn't work, though; the Giants figured out that Clarence Tyler had the ball and they nailed him. We even lost a few yards.

In the huddle, I was next to Clarence and I asked him if he was okay. We were whispering and Eric said, "Shut up, you guys. Here's the play. Slot left . . . 33 Slant . . . on two."

That was the same play where I threw up at practice. I wanted to ask Eric to change his mind and pick another play, but the huddle was over. Everyone clapped and lined up.

The ball was snapped and Eric faked to Clarence and then handed off to me. I held on to it real tight. I tried to find the hole I was supposed to go through, but all I saw was a bunch of bodies and pretty soon all I saw was the ground and there were two Giants on top of me. I thought it was possible that every bone in my body had been crunched by those Giants. But somehow I got up and went back to the huddle. The referee put the ball in the middle of the field at the place I had been tackled. I had carried it for a grand total of one yard. That wasn't anything great, but I thought it was great that at least I was still alive after those Giants had jumped on me and also I didn't fumble or throw up.

The rest of the first half went kind of like that. The Giants never got very far and we never got very far. I thought it was getting boring and I was getting tired of seeing so much of the ground with those Giants on top of me.

Dad gave us a big pep talk at the half and we got to suck on some oranges. In my opinion sucking oranges was the only good part of the whole game.

Then a terrible thing happened on the first play of the second half. I was supposed to carry the ball after Eric pitched it out to me and I got kind of turned around and mixed up. I started running and the Giants weren't there. I ran as fast as I could, holding on to the ball for dear life, and I made it right down to the end zone. I looked up and I thought everyone would be cheering since I had made a touchdown. But all I saw was the Giants jumping up and down and laughing. They just cracked up. The Bears were all groaning. I had forgotten that we had switched directions for the second half, and I had run the wrong way. I made a touchdown, all right. It was for the Giants.

Things didn't get any better, either. I carried the ball a few times after that, and one time I made two yards and one time I fumbled. When that happened the Giants got the ball and scored. I was doing more good for the Giants than I was for the Bears, and when the game was finally over I just wanted to hide somewhere.

A lot of guys were mumbling as we walked off the

field after we lost to the Giants 12–0 and I thought I heard a guy say that the only reason I got to play is 'cause I'm the coach's son.

I went over to Dad who was hanging around talking to some of the parents. "Dad, if you don't mind, I'll just walk home."

"Okay, Norman," he said, and I thought he seemed to be in a bad mood. He was probably mad at me.

I decided to walk home along Rainier Avenue. I was so tired and I just hurt all over from getting jumped on by those Giants.

I passed the pizza place and I thought I might be able to cheer myself up if I went in and played a video game or two. I'm not that great at video games, but I'm not that terrible either. Not like football.

They had a new game in there and it was one I hadn't played before. It was called Berzerk. I decided to try it.

A little man came on the screen and he was in this maze. Then a lot of robots came and started shooting lasers at him. When I moved the lever the man would move and when I pushed a button he would shoot back at the robots. When I moved the little man nearer the robots, the game started talking. It was like the robots were talking in these funny robot voices. "In—tru—der ... In—tru—der ..." it would say.

I was having fun with the game and I was shooting down a lot of the robots when I moved the little man off to one side. "Humanoid is chicken ... Humanoid is chicken," the game said.

I couldn't believe it. I had come in the pizza place

to get cheered up from the stupid football game and now some dumb video game was calling me "chicken."

I was about to leave the pizza place when I looked up and saw that P.W. had come in. He walked over to me.

"Hi, Norman. I was hoping to find you here. I went to watch your game but when I got to the field it was already over."

"You didn't miss anything."

"What happened?"

"I made a touchdown for the other team."

"That's too bad."

"Yeah."

"Wanna play some video games?" he asked.

"I already played Berzerk and the machine started calling me 'chicken.'"

"Oh, that's too bad."

"And I came here to get cheered up."

"Yeah. Well, listen, Norman, I got something to tell you that'll cheer you up."

"Yeah?"

"Yeah." P.W. said, and he started laughing.

"Yeah—well, what?" I asked.

"Well, here's what it is. Our next-door neighbors, the Rileys—well, they just put this hot tub in their backyard."

"Yeah?"

"Yeah, and they get in it naked—right there in the backyard and everything."

"Yeah!"

"Yeah—and you know that tree by my bedroom window?"

"Yeah?"

"Well, when I climb in that tree I can spy on 'em and I can see 'em naked in that hot tub and everything!"

"Yeah! That's really great, P.W."

"Yeah!" Then we started punching each other and laughing and then P.W. asked me if I wanted to come over sometime and get in the tree.

"Yeah!"

P.W. and I left the pizza place and headed home. I sure was glad P.W. was my friend and also because I could go to the garage sales with Carrie and Mr. Koski this afternoon because without them this would have been the worst Saturday of my whole life.

10

"You know, Norman," Dad said when I got home, "I've been thinking—maybe you're cut out to be a defensive player. I'm going to try you at defensive tackle this week at practice."

I said "Okay" and then I went up to my room and changed out of my football stuff. I wish Dad would figure out that I'm not cut out to be a tailback or a defensive tackle or an anything because I'm not cut out to be a football player.

I took a shower and got dressed and left real quick because I didn't want to hang around and talk with Dad about the game. I wanted to get over to Carrie's house as fast as I could.

I walked down 31st Street and when I turned the corner onto Plum Street I saw Carrie out in her yard. She was raking leaves.

"Hi, Carrie."

"Hi, Norman, how was your game?"

That question made me feel terrible but I laughed anyway. "I made a touchdown."

"Great!"

"Not great," I said. "It was for the other team."

"Oh, that's too bad. Well, at least it's over—Gramps said we can go as soon as I finish raking up the yard."

"I'll help you if you want," I said.

"Okay—thanks. I'll get another rake."

Carrie went into the garage and got a rake for me and I started helping her. The leaf pile got bigger and bigger and then for some strange reason, I just felt like jumping in it. Carrie laughed and she jumped in it too and we started throwing leaves at each other and laughing. It was real fun. Then Mr. Koski came out and we raked up the pile again and put the leaves in bags.

As soon as we were done, we all left together for the garage sales. There was one on Hanford Street and one on 29th Street, but by the time we got there most of the stuff was gone.

"I'll tell you what," Mr. Koski said, "let's go back to the house and, Carrie, if your mother is back from the store with the car, I'll take you and Norm to the zoo. I'd sure like to show you the birds."

Carrie and I both liked that idea, and when we got back to her house, her mother was there. She seemed like a nice lady and she made us some lemonade.

"Norm," Mr. Koski said, "would you like to see some of the political buttons from my collection before we go?"

113

"I'd like to," I said, and I followed him and Carrie down to the basement. There was this little room down there and it was filled with all kinds of good merchandise. There were old trunks and a wind-up phonograph and a whole bunch of kites, because I found out that Mr. Koski likes to fly kites. There were beautiful pictures of birds cut out from magazines all over the walls and all kinds of old ship models. Mr. Koski even had a ship in a bottle in that room.

He went over to the trunk and opened it and took out this long box and handed it to me.

I had never seen so many campaign buttons in my life and I had never heard of a single candidate. I guess Mr. Koski liked it that way. There were buttons for John William Davis and Charles Wayland Bryan, Al Smith and Joseph Robinson, Alf Landon and William Knox, Wendell Willkie and Charles McNary, Thomas Dewey and John Bricker, Adlai Stevenson and John Jackson Sparkman, Hubert Horatio Humphrey and Edmund Muskie. Then there were a whole bunch of buttons that said Norman Mattoon Thomas—he must have run for President a lot. Mr. Koski said he had almost all the losing campaigns in his collection since 1920.

"This is a great collection, Mr. Koski," I said, handing him back the box.

"Yep, it sure is, if I do say so myself." Mr. Koski put the box back in the trunk and then we left for the zoo.

We had a great time at the zoo. Mr. Koski knows more about birds than anyone I had ever met. He told Carrie and me all about them. I had never been much of a bird man myself, but listening to Mr. Koski, I could see how a person could get very interested in birds.

After we had seen most of the birds we walked around and looked at a lot of the animals. When we got to the monkeys, Carrie had to go to the bathroom so Mr. Koski and I waited by the monkeys for her. As she left, I said, "Mention my name, and you'll get a good seat," and Carrie thought it was real funny.

I thought it was a good thing that Carrie was gone because there was this one monkey who was sitting there fooling around with himself in front of all the people and all the other monkeys and everything. It was really embarrassing.

Mr. Koski saw it, too, and he said, "You know, Norm, Mark Twain said that he believed that our Heavenly Father invented man because he was disappointed in the monkey—but sometimes I think Mark Twain had it backwards. That little fella there," he said, pointing to the monkey, "seems to be real happy and comfortable about being able to give himself a little pleasure." Then he looked down at me and smiled. "Shall we go find Carrie?"

I said "Sure" and I walked next to Mr. Koski past the monkeys and we met up with Carrie. As I said before, I like Mr. Koski a lot.

On the way home from the zoo, I made up my mind to ask Carrie to go to Seattle Center with me next Saturday after the football game. The only problem was that I just couldn't get up the nerve.

I made up my mind to ask her at school on

Monday, but every time I saw her there was some-one around and I just didn't seem to be able to do it. I even tried to call her up and ask her, but every time I went to the phone I would pick it up and then all of a sudden I would hang up and chicken out. I was beginning to think that video game was right. I was a chicken about life—not just about football.

At practice Dad tried me at defensive tackle, and whenever I tried to block, I ended up just getting practically shoved right off the field.

In the car on the way home from practice Dad said, "You know, Norman, I've been thinking—maybe we should practice kicking this week and then I'll try you out at kicker in the game Saturday."

I just nodded, and when we got home I changed my clothes real quick and got on my bike and rode over to Carrie's house. I was hoping that she might be raking leaves again and that I would see her out in the yard, but she wasn't there.

I rode around the block a few times and then I went over to P.W.'s but he wasn't home, so I went back to Carrie's street and rode around the block some more. On the fifth time I just got off my bike and went up and rang the doorbell.

Carrie opened the door. "Hi, Norman." She seemed kind of surprised.

I didn't seem to be able to make my voice come out right even though I always practice in the shower to make it sound lower—it just squeaked. Finally I just blurted out real quick, "Wanna go to Seattle Center with me Saturday?"

116

"Do you mean me and Gramps?"

"Nope . . . just us, just you and me and we could take the bus and then get the monorail and . . . But we don't have to if you don't want to, I mean . . ." I started wishing I had never come to her house.

"I'd love to, Norman," Carrie said, and she smiled.

"Okay—see you tomorrow," and I waved as I got back on my bike and Carrie shut the door and went back in the house.

I sure felt happy that Carrie wanted to go with me and I almost forgot about the stupid game Saturday.

But I couldn't forget because the rest of the week Dad had me out in the yard trying to turn me into a kicker. He even went out and bought me this little kicking-stand thing to put the ball on.

"Norman, now, don't disappoint me at this position. Above all—a kicker has to concentrate." Dad set up the kicking stand and put the ball carefully on it. "Now, back up and run up to the ball. You should take five steps and then kick, using the top part of your foot and lift the ball with your toe."

I backed up and ran toward the ball.

"Stop!"

"What?" I wondered what I had done wrong.

"Stop! That's not right!" Dad was starting to sound pissed off. "Take your first step with your left foot—so after your five steps you kick on the sixth step with your right foot."

I backed up and started to run again, trying to remember to lead with my left foot and get the steps right.

"Look at the ball, Norman!" Dad yelled. "Concentrate!"

I got to the ball and on the sixth step I kicked the stand. The ball plopped on the ground.

"Norman, you're not trying!"

I did it again and this time I kicked the ball. It went about two feet and landed in the bushes. I kept trying at the kicking but I just wasn't any good. The ball went off to the side most of the time and kept ending up in the bushes.

"Norman, I want you to keep kicking that ball and practice for another half-hour. I'm going in the house now and you stay out here and practice!" Dad yelled at me over his shoulder and then left the yard and went in the house and slammed the door.

I kept practicing kicking the dumb ball and it seemed to me Dad wanted me to be a football player more than anything in the world. He didn't even care so much that I wasn't going to be a running back like him. He just wanted me to be a football player—any kind of football player now.

I woke up real early on Saturday morning. It was still dark and it was raining outside. Everyone else was asleep and the house was quiet. I got dressed and went downstairs.

I got a glass of milk in the kitchen and after I drank it I went to the living room and looked at the trophy case where Dad has all his football awards and stuff. I just stared at it a long time and I got this lump in my throat. Then I made up my mind.

I heard Dad getting up and coming down the stairs. He came in the living room and stood behind me and put his hand on my shoulder. "You know, Son, I always got up early too, the day of a game."

"Dad . . ." I turned around and looked up at him. The house was quiet and all you could hear was the rain on the roof. "Dad . . ."

"What is it, Son?"

"I'm not going to be on the team anymore."

"What?"

"I'm not going to be on the team anymore."

"But the kicker—Norman! Today you were going to try it at kicker."

"Dad, I won't be a good kicker—"

"But you haven't tried yet. It takes a long time to develop the skill. You're just beginning. Norman—this has only been the beginning!"

"I've tried, Dad, I really have. But it's not just kicker or defensive tackle or tailback—"

"What about wide receiver? We haven't tried you at wide receiver yet."

"Dad, I'm not meant to be a football player. You were great, but I'm not. I don't even like it. I like a lot of stuff, but not football—I can't play just for you—it has to be for me, too."

"If we just find the right position . . ."

"No, Dad."

Dad was quiet. He seemed real sad and he looked right at me. "You've thought this over carefully, Norman?"

"Yeah."

"Well, how do you feel if . . . if I keep coaching the Bears and keep working with the other boys?"

"You should, Dad, because it makes you so happy."

Then Dad hugged me and I started crying. He just hugged me for a long time. Finally I told him that I was going back to bed and he said "Okay."

I must have been tired, too, because as soon as I got in bed I fell asleep. When I finally woke up it was still raining and Dad had gone to the game. I got dressed and put on my jacket with the hood and rode over to Carrie's house.

Mr. Koski opened the door. "Well, Norm—didn't expect to see you so early. I thought you had a football game."

"I quit the team, Mr. Koski."

"Well, come on in—no sense in standing there out in the rain. Carrie went to the store with her mother and she should be back before too long."

I followed Mr. Koski into the house and he asked me if I'd like some of his special tea. I went in the kitchen with him and he made the tea. I like Mr. Koski's tea.

"So you decided not to stay on the team," he said while he put the teakettle on.

"Yeah, I feel bad, kind of like I'm a quitter, and I was so scared to tell my Dad—but I just wasn't any good, Mr. Koski, and I didn't like it and I guess it just didn't make sense anymore."

Mr. Koski sat down at the kitchen table. "Well, Norm. Let me tell you. There's all kinds of courage in this world. And I, for one, think you've done a mighty brave thing this morning. Yes siree— mighty brave, because, Norm, I think you were more scared of disappointing your father than you were of going out there and getting your head knocked in. But you faced it all right. Yes, you faced it. You took the chance to tell your father how you really feel."

"I like a lot of things, Mr. Koski. I like garage sales and making fires and making models and hanging out with P.W. and collecting stuff—but not football. I just hope my Dad can understand." Then I got the stupid lump in my throat again.

"Norm, you wait right here. I've got to get something from my trunk and I'll be right back."

While Mr. Koski was in the basement the teakettle started to whistle so I went to the stove and turned it off. When he came back to the kitchen he had a small wooden box with him. He set it down on the table and then went to the stove and fixed the tea.

"Norm, several years ago I bought a trunk at a garage sale. The one I have down in the basement. It was a fine old trunk and it seemed to be empty. When I got it home and looked carefully inside, I found that it had a false bottom and underneath the bottom was this box." Mr. Koski put his hand on the wooden box.

I looked at the box and I wondered what was in it.

"When I got the box open I found these." Mr. Koski opened the box and inside I saw a whole bunch of shiny medals. They were made of beautiful silver and gold and they had colored ribbons attached to them.

"Now, I looked at them closely and I could see that they had some writing in a foreign language. It wasn't anything I recognized, but after some research I discovered that these medals were from

Liechtenstein—yes, Liechtenstein, that tiny little country near Switzerland. These medals, as far as I could tell, seemed to be the highest honors of the Liechtenstein government or army—although I never did find out if they have an army."

I looked in the box and I thought those medals were the most beautiful things I had ever seen.

"Well, I was sure someone would be missing something so special, but the problem was I couldn't remember which garage sale I had bought the trunk at. When I finally figured it out and went back to the house, the people had moved." Mr. Koski got up and poured himself another cup of tea.

"Well, I decided right then and there that since I had ended up with these medals that I should never sell 'em or anything like that just because the silver and gold would be worth something. Nope—I decided that I'd give 'em out whenever I saw an everyday act of human courage."

Then Mr. Koski reached in the box and took out one of the medals. "Norm, this is only the second time I've done this, but I think you've earned this today. Some folks go their whole lives before they find the courage to tell their folks who they are and nothing was as frightening to you then as the thought of letting your father down." Mr. Koski leaned over and pinned the medal on my shirt.

"Thanks a lot, Mr. Koski."

Then Mr. Koski shook my hand.

"Who got the medal the first time?" I asked him.

"Well, I'm glad you asked me that. The first time I awarded one of the medals was to Miss Nettie

O'Malley. Nettie O'Malley is a bit older than I am, she's eighty-two. I first got to know Nettie down at the Pike Place Market where I would often see her. Nettie has no family left, none at all. She lives all alone in a small apartment near the market. And Nettie doesn't have much money, she just lives on her Social Security is all. But what Nettie does is just keep going. Yep, she gets up every day and goes to the market. She talks to her friends who sell vegetables and she buys a few things for her dinner. Nettie goes home at night and fixes her dinner. She sits down in front of the TV and she sits where it's warm right next to the radiator. And every day—rain or shine—Nettie gets one fresh flower from the market that she puts in a little vase right by her dinner. Now, that may not sound like courage to some people, Norm. But Nettie O'Malley knows how to keep going. And sometimes, Norm—when you're old and alone—that takes a lot of courage."

I liked hearing about Miss Nettie O'Malley and the way Mr. Koski told it she seemed like a brave person to me and I was real proud that Mr. Koski thought I was as brave as Miss Nettie O'Malley.

Carrie and her Mom came home and we got ready to leave for Seattle Center. Mr. Koski told them about the medal and how I got it and I was kind of embarrassed, but I didn't mind too much. Carrie thought it was real neat and so did her Mom.

I wasn't sure what to talk about on the way downtown on the bus and at first Carrie and I didn't say much.

Finally I said, "Hey, Carrie—what did one frog say to the other?"

"I don't know. What?"

"Time's sure fun when you're having flies."

Carrie laughed a lot. She really liked the frog joke and I thought we were off to a pretty good start.

When we got to Seattle Center I bought us some cotton candy and Carrie would take some off her stick and put it in my mouth. It was fun. We went on a bunch of the rides in the Fun Forest and then we both decided to get on the Ferris wheel.

We climbed in and we went a little ways up and then it would stop while they put people in below us. Finally it was all full and we went round and round.

I don't know exactly how it happened because I never did do the sneeze thing, but somehow I just got my arm around Carrie. At first I was afraid she might say "Yuk," but she didn't—in fact, she squished even closer to me.

"This is fun, Norman," Carrie said and she leaned her head next to mine.

"Call me Norm," I said and I leaned even closer to her.

If you want to know the truth, I could have stayed on that Ferris wheel with Carrie Koski forever. But pretty soon the ride was over and it was time to go home.

When we got back to the neighborhood, I walked Carrie to the door and we said we'd see each other Monday.

I still had on the medal Mr. Koski gave me and as I walked down Plum Street I kept looking down at it. I decided to stop over at P.W.'s house on the way home and tell him about the medal.

On the way I jumped in a big leaf pile for the fun of it and I also started to whistle a song we had heard on the Ferris wheel. It sure had been a good day for me, Norman Schnurman, son of Mad Dog.